MW00461944

MAGIC

AND THE

LAW OF

ATTRACTION

A Witch's Guide to the Magic of Intention, Raising Your Frequency, and Building Your Reality

LISA CHAMBERLAIN

Magic and the Law of Attraction

Published by **Chamberlain Publications**

ISBN-13: 978-1-912715-76-3

Disclaimer

No part of this publication may be reproduced or transmitted in any form or by any means, mechanical or electronic, including photocopying or recording, or by any information storage and retrieval system, or transmitted by email without permission in writing from the publisher.

While all attempts have been made to verify the information provided in this publication, neither the author nor the publisher assumes any responsibility for errors, omissions, or contrary interpretations of the subject matter herein.

This book is for entertainment purposes only. The views expressed are those of the author alone, and should not be taken as expert instruction or commands. The reader is responsible for his or her own actions.

Adherence to all applicable laws and regulations, including international, federal, state, and local governing professional licensing, business practices, advertising, and all other aspects of doing business in the US, Canada, or any other jurisdiction is the sole responsibility of the purchaser or reader.

Neither the author nor the publisher assumes any responsibility or liability whatsoever on the behalf of the purchaser or reader of these materials.

Any perceived slight of any individual or organization is purely unintentional.

YOUR FREE GIFT

Thank you for adding this book to your Wiccan library! To learn more, why not join Lisa's Wiccan community and get an exclusive, free spell book?

The book is a great starting point for anyone looking to try their hand at practicing magic. The ten beginner-friendly spells can help you to create a positive atmosphere within your home, protect yourself from negativity, and attract love, health, and prosperity.

Little Book of Spells is now available to read on your laptop, phone, tablet, Kindle or Nook device!

To download, simply visit the following link:

www.wiccaliving.com/bonus

GET THREE
FREE AUDIOBOOKS
FROM LISA CHAMBERLAIN

Did you know that all of Lisa's books are available in audiobook format? Best of all, you can get **three audiobooks completely free** as part of a 30-day trial with Audible.

Wicca Starter Kit contains three of Lisa's most popular books for beginning Wiccans, all in one convenient place. It's the best and easiest way to learn more about Wicca while also taking audiobooks for a spin! Simply visit:

www.wiccaliving.com/free-wiccan-audiobooks

Alternatively, *Spellbook Starter Kit* is the ideal option for building your magical repertoire using candle and color magic, crystals and mineral stones, and magical herbs. Three spellbooks —over 150 spells—are available in one free volume, here:

www.wiccaliving.com/free-spell-audiobooks

Audible members receive free audiobooks every month, as well as exclusive discounts. It's a great way to experiment and see if audiobook learning works for you.

If you're not satisfied, you can cancel anytime within the trial period. You won't be charged, and you can still keep your books!

CONTENTS

INTRODUCTION

If you're reading this book, there's a good chance you've already heard about the Law of Attraction.

Maybe it came to your attention through the movie *The Secret*, or the best-selling book of the same title, or any of the literally hundreds of available books on the topic. You may have even heard the Law of Attraction mentioned on television, as it has made its way into mainstream culture over the past several years.

Indeed, scores of "self-help" authors and speakers have made an effort to promote their own interpretations of this most basic concept of how the Universe operates: *like attracts like*.

This seemingly simple aphorism is applied to the realm of the human mind, as we are told that our thoughts are actually creating our reality, and that to change our lives we need to change our thinking.

Depending on the source, the Law of Attraction may be discussed in spiritual or religious terms, or it may be presented from a secular point of view. The more mainstream, "pop culture" books tend to focus on its applications for financial success, which is no real surprise, given the materialistic culture we're living in.

However, there are also authors who understand that there's more to life than money, and offer approaches and strategies for bringing success to all areas of our lives. We can use the focused energy of our thoughts to bring about the healing of illness, more loving relationships, and the accomplishment of long-held goals and dreams, in addition to financial prosperity.

Of course, skeptics will argue that if the Law of Attraction was real, we'd have all implemented it into our lives on a grand scale already, and wouldn't need to keep reading books about it. It's true that the implications of "like attracts like," or to put it more concretely, *thoughts become things*, are not necessarily easy to instantly put into practice. But if it didn't work for anyone, why would it still be such a popular topic?

Interestingly, a growing number of authors have been connecting the phenomenon of the Law of Attraction to emerging discoveries in the field of quantum physics—including some of the quantum scientists themselves.

Our understanding of the nature of physical reality has radically shifted over the past several years, with experiments revealing that everything is essentially malleable at the most fundamental "subatomic" level, that all matter is interconnected, and that the simple act of *observing* an object can affect its physical makeup.

While most scientists will remind us that these discoveries remain theoretical and have not been connected to reality as we know it in any practical way, the implications are hard to ignore for those who understand that when it comes to "reality," there is *always* more going on than meets the eye!

The Law of Attraction may seem like a recent phenomenon, but it actually has quite a long history. It has been presented by writers and thinkers from several different spiritual, philosophical, and occult backgrounds over the centuries. In fact, many claim that the concepts underlying the Law of Attraction have been understood for thousands of years, going all the way back to sources from ancient Egypt.

It has been used as a framework for understanding magic by many practitioners of occult arts, including Wiccans and other Witches. It has also been embraced by many Christians over the past two centuries, who have cited specific Bible passages to underscore their own understanding of the relationship between mind and matter.

It may seem odd to some that people from such apparently contradictory spiritual traditions could share the same concept, but given that this is very ancient wisdom, it's not so unthinkable that it could show up in a wide variety of places.

Do you have to be "religious" or "spiritual" to believe in and work with the Law of Attraction? No. But you do have to have an open mind, and accept that what you've been taught about the world and how reality works has come from an incomplete understanding.

This is something that practicing Wiccans and other Witches (not all of whom identify as "spiritual," by the way) have long known. And while a Witch's understanding of the workings of the Universe is much more complex than the simple axiom of "thoughts become things," the concepts inherent to magic and Witchcraft can be a very useful lens through which to truly understand how we can manifest positive change in our lives.

This guide is an introduction to the Law of Attraction from a Witch's point of view, but you don't have to be a Witch in order to gain plenty of insight in these pages. It's actually intended for both Witches and non-Witches alike.

Maybe you practice Wicca or another form of Witchcraft but have never been formally introduced to the Law of Attraction. Or, maybe you have discovered it in some mainstream sources, but can't quite figure out how to make it work for you.

You might even be curious about both Witchcraft and the Law of Attraction, but have remained too skeptical of magic to really explore its possibilities—if this is the case, you're definitely not alone, and this guide will likely help you move closer to opening that door. But whether or not you ever intend to try any magic, the concepts and suggested practices presented here can get you a long way toward making your goals a reality.

We'll begin with a basic, "secular" overview of the Law of Attraction as it has been discussed in many sources over the past several decades, while also taking a look at its ancient roots and its parallels in modern science.

Then we'll examine these concepts from the point of view of people who practice Witchcraft, which will help you see the bigger picture that most mainstream sources don't include in their discussions, as well as the parallels between applying the Law of Attraction to your life and the practice of magic.

Finally, we'll take a closer look at how both Witches and non-Witches alike can truly begin to shift their thoughts and retrain their minds in order to attract successful outcomes in any area of life they wish to improve.

And since no single source on the Law of Attraction is ever likely to be enough to get you all the way to where you want to go, you'll find a list of suggested reading at the end of this guide, with sources from both within and outside of the Witching world.

So read on, keep your mind open, and enjoy the journey!

PART ONE

WHAT IS THE LAW OF ATTRACTION?

THE POWER
OF THE MIND

You've almost certainly heard the expression "You can do anything you put your mind to." Or how about "mind over matter"?

Experts in medicine, sports, business, and other fields have long known that the human mind—and the focused use of its powers—can have a tremendous effect on our physical bodies, emotional well-being, financial success, and just about any area of life we can think of. For example, we know that people who perform physically—like athletes and dancers—must first visualize the complex movements and challenging physical feats that their bodies are then able to enact.

It has also been shown that people who have a high degree of self-confidence project it outwardly and are treated differently by others than people who exhibit poor self-confidence.

And we even know that our general outlook counts for a lot when it comes to quality of life. After all, constant complaining makes it hard to notice (and therefore experience) the blessings in one's daily life, while those with a "default mode" of gratitude and appreciation are less emotionally affected by hardship.

With very rare exceptions, everyone has had the experience of a truly "bad day," in which everything seems to be working against them. Perhaps it starts with a spilled cup of coffee in the car on the way to work, followed by terrible traffic, difficulty finding a parking spot, a grouchy coworker, a conflict with a customer or client, and several unexpected obstacles to completing our tasks—all before lunch!

At some point during a day like this, most of us are bound to simply "accept" that we're having a "bad day," and then start expecting more mishaps to befall us before the day is over. Many of us are likely to start verbalizing this conclusion to our co-workers. "I'm having a bad day," we'll say. And then when the boss asks us to stay late for an unscheduled meeting, we'll add it to our list of evidence to support our conclusion.

When we finally get home, we may tell our roommates, partner, or spouse all about our day, remembering every instance of bad luck, and nodding as our companions validate our assessment of it as a "bad" one. And while this venting may feel like a relief, at least in the moment, we're unlikely to feel much better about our experience, because as long as we're still paying attention to the unpleasant aspects of this day, we're keeping those unpleasant feelings alive and active.

The good news is that more often than not, a good night's sleep will put a stop to this negative momentum, and we're likely to have a better day tomorrow.

While almost everyone will experience at least one day similar to the one described above, not many people understand that this is a classic illustration of the Law of Attraction at work in our lives.

The Law of Attraction, simply put, is the phenomenon of "like attracting like," and it applies to how we think, in every moment of every day, no matter what is happening to us or around us. Another way of putting it is "you get what you think about," or, as many writers on the subject have said, "thoughts become things."

This isn't to say that you are *consciously* causing the specific circumstances that are plaguing you on a "bad day"—the spilled coffee was truly an accident, and you certainly weren't expecting to have to stay at work after hours.

However, when you *focus* on the spilled coffee, allowing it to cause you frustration and other negative feelings, you are opening up an invisible door to let in more circumstances that will feed that negativity. And the more you vocalize these feelings to yourself and others, by saying "I'm having a bad day" and recounting all of the occurrences that reinforce this notion in your own mind, the more you will attract additional circumstances to confirm these feelings.

This is why the good night's sleep is so important—once you're asleep, you stop thinking about your bad day, and therefore stop attracting more negative occurrences!

Many people, when discovering the Law of Attraction for the first time, are not pleased by the idea that their own negativity might be responsible for a bad day. But the good news here is that once you accept this premise, it becomes equally possible to have a "good day"—by focusing on the things that are going well, rather than the things that aren't.

When you focus on what's working out for you, you attract more circumstances that bring you joy and excitement. And, just as importantly, when you have this positive focus you aren't as easily knocked off-kilter by any less-than-pleasant experiences.

For example, everyone has experienced at least one day in their lives where the weather is so enjoyable that no ordinary unpleasant occurrences can bring them down.

Maybe it's a bright, sunny spring morning after a long winter, when you can finally leave for work without your heavy jacket. If you're focused on this feeling of being free from the cold, and anticipating the beauty of the trees coming into bloom and birds beginning to chirp, you're sending out a signal that causes more positive phenomena to come into your awareness.

Now, it's still perfectly possible that you might spill your coffee in the car. However, staying focused on the positive will allow you to consciously decide not to let it bother you. The spilled coffee doesn't have to set you off on a path of anxiety, anger, or any other negative feelings. After all, you can't un-spill it, so focusing on it doesn't solve anything.

Instead, you can keep your attention trained on the beauty of the day and the overall happiness of your mood. And the longer you can keep your positive energy flowing, the more likely it is that you'll have a great day—smooth traffic, easy parking, pleasant exchanges with coworkers, etc.—and a lovely evening spent feeling grateful for all of the things that have been going well for you.

One interesting way to test the power of the mind is to watch what happens when you or someone around you says "I'm coming down with a cold." Because we understand that viruses tend to be transmitted from person to person, we often assume that if someone in our household or workplace is sick, we are likely to contract the illness as well. It's only a matter of time, we think to ourselves, and start mentally preparing to be sick.

If we fully believe that this is the logical order of events, we will almost certainly "come down with" whatever it is that's going around, as we're essentially telling our own bodies to start feeling lousy.

If, instead, we maintain a focus on how well we actually feel in the moment, and tell ourselves to expect to remain healthy, we have a far greater chance of dodging the virus, no matter how many people around us have caught it. Of course, it helps to take extra measures to stay healthy—maybe by upping our intake of vitamin C, brewing some Echinacea tea, and avoiding unnecessary stress—but the focus needs to be on wellness, as opposed to a fear of illness.

This crucial mind-body connection can be seen in the phenomenon known as the "placebo effect," which occurs in medical studies when subjects are given sugar pills in place of actual medication and get better anyway. Because they believe they have what they need to heal from their illness, their bodies respond positively, without any actual medical intervention.

Perhaps the most important thing to realize about the Law of Attraction is that it is at work all the time, in every aspect of your life, whether you are consciously aware of it or not.

Your attitudes, your outlook, and even your unconscious underlying beliefs about what is possible for you are attracting circumstances, people, and other physical manifestations into your life that match those thoughts.

So if you decide that you're having a bad day, experiences that match this belief will continue to show up all day long. Conversely, when you think and feel positively, you will attract positive experiences.

This isn't to say, however, that it's easy or automatic to just stop thinking negative thoughts. This shift is a difficult one to make for most people, and especially for those who are dealing with major challenges, such as severe health issues, mounting financial problems, or a job that makes them miserable on a daily basis. When you're constantly faced with circumstances that feel negative, it can seem next to impossible to come up with anything truly positive to think about.

But no matter what your life may be like today, you *can* choose, right now, to start observing the way you respond to what's happening, and be open to making significant changes to your ingrained habits of thought. Indeed, rather than letting what you're experiencing dictate how you think, you can start to *choose* your thoughts according to what you want to experience.

THREE CORE METHODS FOR WORKING WITH THE LAW OF ATTRACTION

Among the multitudes of books about the Law of Attraction, you will find authors offering many different approaches to creating this change in how you think. Depending on who you are and what your orientation to the world has been like up until this point, some strategies may make more sense than others.

Because there are so many different kinds of people, it makes sense that there should be so many different methods for learning and applying these concepts. Nonetheless, many of these sources have in common three core methods for making the necessary shift to a positive outlook on your current life and your future potential: **appreciation**, **affirmation**, and **visualization**.

Appreciation, also commonly referred to as gratitude, is a focus on what is going well for you, whether you're focusing on the immediate present moment, or on your life in general. When we make a point of listing and recognizing the positive in our lives, we are automatically shifting our attention away from the negative, putting ourselves in a place to attract more of what we appreciate.

Many experts on the Law of Attraction recommend establishing a daily practice of recognizing as many positive attributes as you can, no matter how seemingly small—a delicious breakfast, a nice hot shower, or hearing your favorite song on the radio— and actively feeling appreciation for these things.

Affirmation is the act of repeating positive statements, whether silently or out loud, that describe the reality we're looking to create.

For example, if you're looking to increase your financial well-being, you might create an affirmation like this: "I have everything I need and more for a secure, abundant life." If you're seeking a relationship, you might say "I am in a healthy, loving relationship with my perfect match."

This can be a challenging practice for many, because while appreciation involves focusing on what's right in front of you, affirmation requires a willingness to "fake it till you make it" by pretending that you have already manifested your goals. It often feels somewhat silly at first, but many people have found that through repeated practice, over time, their affirmations do become their reality.

Visualization, as you might expect, is the practice of creating mental pictures of the circumstances we desire. You spend time imagining the house you want to live in, the dream job you're seeking, or the state of health you're looking to achieve.

The goal of visualization is to create a vivid sense of your dreams coming true, but it involves more than just being able to see it in your mind's eye—you also need to create the *feeling* of having achieved your desire, because this is what really begins the process of turning your thoughts into things.

This can be challenging if you've been accustomed to picturing what you want, while at the same time feeling down about not having it. The objective is not to pine away for something that feels out of reach, but to imagine it as clearly as possible while believing that it will come to you.

Interestingly, the practice of magic also involves all three of these processes, and we'll take a closer look at how Witches incorporate them later on in this guide.

But for now, just keep this in mind: if you make a commitment to changing your habits of thought, you will soon be able to shake off that spilled cup of coffee first thing in the morning, and head off what would have been, before your discovery of the Law of Attraction, a "bad day."

And if you keep up the practice of shifting those thoughts, over time you will manifest positive changes in your life that you would never have thought possible before.

THE HISTORY
OF AN IDEA

Many thousands of people—perhaps even millions—have made amazing improvements in their lives through applying the basic principles of the Law of Attraction.

But where did this "Law" come from? Who discovered it? And how exactly does it work? There are various answers to these questions, and several schools of thought about how to put it into practice.

Depending on your background, your particular orientation to the world, and your degree of skepticism about this idea that "thoughts become things," some sources, writers, and teachings may be more accessible or seem more credible than others.

This guide will ultimately focus on the Law of Attraction from the perspective of people who integrate it into the practice of magic, but before we jump into the Witching world, let's take a brief tour of the history of this concept as it's been defined and explained over the past two centuries.

THE
NOT-SO-SECRET "SECRET"

Probably the most widely-known introduction to the Law of Attraction has been *The Secret*, a 2006 movie produced by an Australian television producer named Rhonda Byrne who became interested in the Law of Attraction after reading *The Science of Getting Rich*, written nearly 100 years earlier by Wallace Wattles. Wattles' book outlines the changes in thought and action needed to attract wealth into one's life, including focusing on gratitude for what one already has.

Byrne had been very down on her luck in many respects and was inspired to research what she came to call "the secret," suddenly seeing how it was at work in the lives of famous philosophers, artists, scientists, and other successful people throughout history.

As she delved into further explorations, she found herself connecting with several contemporary "New Age" thinkers, writers, and teachers from many fields, ranging from entrepreneurs and success coaches to quantum physicists and philosophers, each with their own wisdom regarding the Law of Attraction and its implications for living a consciously-created life. In *The Secret*, more than 20 of these teachers share their ideas and explain how their understandings can be applied to shaping every area of our lives.

Originally conceived as a TV special in Australia, the project ultimately became a full-length documentary, and later a book, that gained widespread attention from mainstream audiences, grossing more than $300 million in sales. This very positive reception was no doubt a result of Byrne's very positive energy and enthusiasm for sharing the news of the Law of Attraction.

For all the hype around it, however, *The Secret* is not without some significant flaws. Many of its critics argue that it presents an over-simplified, surface understanding of the Law of Attraction.

We'll revisit this observation later on, but first let's examine the rather fanciful premise of the title: the notion that the knowledge of the Law of Attraction had actually been purposely kept secret for thousands of years, as if locked away in a vault, with only a privileged few having access to its wisdom as it was periodically discovered, then hidden again, then stolen and recovered periodically throughout history.

The Secret claims to be only now presenting it to the masses for the first time ever. This was essentially a marketing ploy, and not true in any literal sense, since plenty of people have been working with the Law of Attraction for at least the past 150 years. In fact, there is a long tradition of authors and teachers reaching out openly with their knowledge.

"NEW THOUGHT" IN A "NEW AGE"

Most observers of this latest round of attention to the Law of Attraction trace its roots to the beginnings of the New Thought movement. This was a philosophical movement that began in the United States in the late 19th century, at a time when many writers and thinkers were exploring alternative ideas about religion and the nature of reality.

One of the core beliefs that developed during this time was that all disease has a mental cause at its source, and that therefore the proper use of "right thinking" can heal the body. Another is that everything in the universe is suffused with "Infinite Intelligence," or, as many referred to it, "God."

While the movement was influenced to some extent by elements of Hinduism as well as occult studies— Hermeticism in particular, which we will examine next—it largely evolved within a Christian context.

Several of these writers blended a kind of Christian mysticism with a rational approach to thinking and acting to create ideal conditions in one's life, leading to different but related schools of thought known as Christian Science, Divine Science, and other variations. However, not all New Thought participants focused on a religious connection, and the labels "New Thought" and "Christian Science" emerged largely to distinguish the religious from the secular camps within the movement.

New Thought is said to have grown out of the teachings of a well-known healer, philosopher and inventor named Phineas Quimby, who taught in the early 1800s about the impact of the mind on the health of the body. While he didn't use the phrase "Law of Attraction," his message was essentially that once the mind was properly refocused on the belief that the body is healthy, disease would be cured.

Over the next several decades, others who subscribed to this idea would develop it further to apply to all areas of life, as opposed to just health. By the end of the 19th century, many New Thought writers were citing the Law of Attraction in what we now call "self-help" books, focused on retraining the mind in order to succeed at any goal.

A few of the most well-known of these books were *In Tune With the Infinite* (1897) by Ralph Trine, *Thoughts are Things* (1897) by Prentice Mulford, and *Thought Vibration or the Law of Attraction in the Thought World* (1906) by William Walker Atkinson.

The popular titles of the early 20th century brought a bigger emphasis to the realm of financial prosperity, such as Bruce MacLelland's *Prosperity Through Thought Force* (1907), Wallace Wattles' *The Science of Getting Rich* (1910), and Napoleon Hill's classic *Think and Grow Rich* (1937).

All of these authors offered their own approaches to deliberately training the mind to focus on the positive, through gratitude and appreciation, and channel this positive energy into inspired action and the realization of one's goals.

Although it seems that New Thought and the Law of Attraction may have fallen out of style during the middle of the 20th century, the core principles never truly disappeared, and the thought-directed approach to living well was revived by many spiritual and philosophical writers in what became known as the New Age movement.

Beginning in the 1970s, the label "New Age" has been applied to a very broad set of ideas, philosophies, including metaphysics, occult traditions like astrology and Tarot, and many different concepts of spirituality, all of which reject the organized and doctrine-centered nature of traditional monotheistic religions like Christianity.

The term is so broad that it's common for just about any idea that is not thoroughly grounded in Western science to be called "New Age," and many people with interests that are considered "New Age" by mainstream culture actually reject the title.

(Interestingly, Wicca and other forms of Witchcraft are generally considered to be part of the "New Age" phenomenon, even though these belief systems predate the movement by several decades—or, as many would argue, by centuries. Nonetheless, there's plenty of overlap between the two, which can be seen by visiting just about any shop identifying as "New Age" or "metaphysical.")

One of the most well-known authors of this newer incarnation of "New Thought" is Louise Hay, who published *Heal Your Body* in 1976, which, like Phineas Quimby's work, focused on using the power of the mind to overcome illness. Hay herself used positive affirmations, visualizations, and other non-medically invasive techniques to cure herself of cancer. Later, she applied her approach beyond physical healing to all areas of life in *You Can Heal Your Life* (1984).

Inspirational writer, speaker, and teacher Wayne Dyer was another key figure, who wrote dozens of books promoting the ability of every individual to manifest desires, including *You'll See It When You Believe It* (2001), *The Power of Intention* (2005), and *Change Your Thoughts, Change Your Life* (2009).

While the phrase "Law of Attraction" may not always appear explicitly in the works of these authors, the central connection between one's thoughts and one's reality is found throughout the genre.

Perhaps the most comprehensive body of work involving the Law of Attraction comes from a source known as Abraham, a group of non-physical entities whose collective teachings are delivered through a woman named Esther Hicks.

Hicks had had no real experience with New Age philosophy before discovering meditation, which she began to practice after meeting her husband, Jerry Hicks. Several months into her new practice, Esther discovered that something from the invisible realm was attempting to communicate with her. As she learned to open up and fine-tune her receptivity, she and Jerry began what ultimately became a decades-long dialogue with this "infinite intelligence," which is how they define what they came to call "Abraham."

Through books, recordings, and live seminars which are broadcast all over the globe, Hicks translates Abraham's teachings on the nature of consciousness, the interconnectivity of non-physical and physical reality, and the obstacles to success that we create for ourselves through our everyday habits of thought.

The Abraham approach centers on using emotions as your guide to creating better circumstances in your life: focus on thoughts that feel good to think about, and ignore the thoughts that don't. By consistently practicing attentiveness to how your thoughts make you feel and learning to consciously shift the negative thoughts, you eventually diminish what you don't want to experience and increase what you do want.

A few of the most popular Abraham books, co-written by Esther and Jerry Hicks, are *Ask and It Is Given: Learning to Manifest Your Desires* (2005), *The Amazing Power of Deliberate Intent: Living the Art of Allowing* (2006), and *The Astonishing Power of Emotions* (2007).

THE NEXT STEPS

As we have seen, the Law of Attraction has been available to the masses as a concept, in one form or another, for at least over two hundred years, despite some claims that it's a "new" discovery.

However, there are plenty of people—including many who practice Witchcraft—who know that its principles have actually been studied and implemented over several centuries, thanks to a wisdom tradition dating back thousands of years.

Hermeticism, a diverse collection of esoteric, spiritual, and philosophical studies with origins in ancient Egypt, is widely considered to include the original source of the Law of Attraction, where it sits within a broader, multidimensional framework for understanding how and why "like attracts like."

In Part Two, we'll examine this framework from a Witch's perspective, but first, let's take a look at the basic ideas that relate directly to the Law of Attraction as it is often presented in mainstream sources. We'll also explore how these concepts have found parallels in the most cutting-edge science of today.

ANCIENT MYSTICISM AND MODERN SCIENCE

For the last few hundred years, mainstream Western culture has generally perceived science and spirituality as separate realms. While spiritual or "occult" pursuits involve a belief in the mysterious and the unseen, modern science is firmly grounded in the pursuit of tangible proof.

This split between the two has been reinforced as more and more advances in scientific inquiry and technological development have provided answers to questions that used to have no "rational" answers.

For example, a few centuries ago, illness was often considered to be the result of a curse, but as we came to discover bacteria and viruses, these suspicions became a thing of the past. And it's been a very long time since it was commonly believed that thunder is caused by the anger of the gods, now that we know about electricity and the makeup of clouds.

Still, science continues to confront mysteries, and we're still a long way off from understanding everything there is to know about the Universe.

What many people may not realize is that what we now recognize as the scientific method was initially brought into being through insights that originated in ancient civilizations—in other words, when discovery and experimentation were rooted in mysticism and the spiritual infused every aspect of human existence.

And while much of this knowledge was lost or ignored for several centuries between the fall of the Roman Empire and the end of the Middle Ages, it was rediscovered and further developed during the European Renaissance—the same time that the rise of science began to accelerate.

One particular tradition of ancient knowledge has been shown to have an influence on early Christian writers and Renaissance philosophers alike. Known as **Hermeticism**, it included philosophy as well as alchemy, astrology, and other elements of occult studies. Tenets of Hermeticism can be seen in the work of Copernicus, Francis Bacon, and Newton, as well as the 19th-century British occult movement— which had parallels with the American New Thought movement, where the Law of Attraction gained particular attention.

THE KYBALION AND
THE HERMETIC PRINCIPLES

The core teachings of Hermeticism are centered around a body of writing attributed to an ancient Egyptian called Hermes Trismegistus. This figure was said to be a priest of the god Toth, who was associated with magic, writing, and wisdom.

Hermes Trismegistus was believed to have written his works sometime before 300 B.C., though some historians date them a few centuries later. There is some uncertainty as to whether he was an actual person, or a god who was given credit by anonymous authors for their work. Either way, the teachings from this source were clearly powerful enough to last through the ages.

Cropping up in one form or another from the 1500s through the end of the 1800s, Hermeticism emerged into the 20th century in the form of a mysterious book called the *Kybalion.* Published in 1908, by authors known only as "Three Initiates," the *Kybalion* outlined key ideas in the work of Hermes Trismegistus (to whom the book is dedicated) with a mission of bringing "arcane knowledge" to a contemporary audience.

(Interestingly, the authors claim that this knowledge had long been kept hidden from the wider world, passed down secretly through the generations by the initiated few. Whether or not there is any truth in this, it could certainly be the inspiration for the similar claim in *The Secret*.)

Because the text is clearly influenced by later occult studies, the book itself is identified by scholars as "neo-Hermeticism," but the basic framework it lays out, known today as the Hermetic Principles, is rooted in the older teachings. As to the true authorship of the *Kybalion*, many guesses have been made by scholars, but the most plausible claim is that it was written by William Walker Atkinson (the author of *Thought Vibration or the Law of Attraction in the Thought World*), perhaps collaboratively with others in the New Thought movement.

The Hermetic Principles—often referred to as the Hermetic Laws—are a set of seven core tenets that explain the intricate ways in which the Universe functions at the most basic level. These principles have been identified in teachings within various ancient spiritual and philosophical traditions, not just within Egypt, but in ancient Greece and Indian Vedic philosophy as well.

The *Kybalion* states that through an understanding and application of these principles, students can learn to transform their mental state in such a way that will bring forth changes in the conditions of their lives.

The phrase "Law of Attraction" appears just once in the text, described as an aspect of the Principle of Cause and Effect, but it is related to several of the seven principles, which are themselves interrelated. Two others in particular—the Principle of Correspondence and the Principle of Vibration—are key for gaining a deeper understanding of the Law of Attraction than what is provided in many mainstream sources.

The **Principle of Correspondence** is presented in the Kybalion in a simple phrase: "as above, so below; as below, so above."

The Universe is described as having three general "planes" of existence, or "three great classes of phenomena," which are collectively called the "Three Great Planes," and individually identified as physical, mental, and spiritual. While linear time as we experience it exists on the physical plane, it does not exist on the others, which contain dimensions we are unable to perceive from our human perspectives.

Later in the text, the three planes are each divided into seven sub-planes which are described in more detail. The planes are not wholly separate from each other, but rather are said to "shade into each other," each having influence on the others. The axiom "as above, so below" tells us that what is true on a higher plane is also true on the lower plane.

Another way to view it is that the Universe is the macrocosm, while Earth is the microcosm, and what exists in one must necessarily exist in the other. Because the different planes of existence "shade" or blend into each other, the physical world is interacting with the non-physical. This is the connection by which thought, which is non-physical, influences circumstances, which occur in the physical world.

If you, standing on the physical plane, send an intention into the non-physical, it will exist there. Then, it must eventually become manifest in the physical, because the higher plane must be replicated on the lower plane—"as above, so below." This is one element of how the Law of Attraction functions in our reality.

Another crucial component is the **Principle of Vibration**, which states that "nothing rests; everything moves; everything vibrates."

All matter is composed of energy, and every particle in existence is in constant motion in the form of vibration, no matter how stationary the *object* made up of the particles appears to be. Walls, furniture, and every other presumably solid manifestation of matter is simply vibrating at such a low frequency that we can't perceive it, and therefore we experience solid objects as being still. (By contrast, we can see the movement of matter in liquid form, as well as in gaseous form when the gaseous substance is visible.)

However, it's not just physical matter that vibrates, but non-physical energy as well. Thoughts, which exist on the mental plane, are part of non-physical energy. Therefore every thought you think has its own vibration, which in turn has an effect on your overall emotional (and, consequently, physical) vibration.

The frequencies of these vibrations, and their resulting effects, depend on the nature of the thoughts. Positive thoughts vibrate at higher frequencies and feel better to focus on, while thoughts at lower frequencies feel less pleasant or even painful. And though there are millions of other vibrations occurring in our physical bodies, our overall, dominant vibration is matching the frequencies of our dominant thoughts.

Now, when we remember that "like attracts like" according to the Law of Attraction, we can see that vibrations attract other vibrations at similar frequencies. When we put this together with the knowledge that all planes of existence—both physical and nonphysical—influence each other, we can begin to see how it can be so easy to experience a string of unpleasant occurrences that we ultimately attribute to "having a bad day." Conversely, positive thoughts attract positive experiences because the person having the thoughts is *vibrating at the right frequency to attract the positive experience.*

The third Hermetic Principle that relates directly to the Law of Attraction is the **Law of Cause and Effect.**

The *Kybalion* explains that "Every Cause has its Effect; every Effect has its Cause; everything happens according to Law."

This may seem at first to be fairly self-explanatory. After all, we understand the concept of cause and effect as it relates to specific phenomena. If you drop a bowling ball from a third-story window, it will fall very quickly and break apart when it hits the sidewalk below. If you leave your car's headlights on for long enough when the car isn't running, the battery will need to be recharged before the car will start again.

These cause-and-effect sequences are easy to connect, because we can identify the actions that led to the consequences. On the other hand, when something happens that we *can't* easily explain—an amazing winning streak at the casino or a freak storm that no meteorologist saw coming—many people tend to chalk it up to "good" or "bad" luck.

But the Principle of Cause and Effect negates this notion. The *Kybalion* states that "Chance is but a name for Law not recognized; there are many planes of causation, but nothing escapes the Law."

In other words, while many effects that we observe on the physical plane have identifiable causes on the physical plane, such as the examples of the bowling ball and the car battery, we also experience countless effects with causes on the mental and spiritual planes.

This is because, like all the other Hermetic Principles, Cause and Effect applies on all planes of reality. Your thoughts, existing on the mental plane, cause effects that eventually manifest on the physical plane, whether you recognize the causal relationship or not.

Ultimately, the cause of everything we experience in the world "outside" of ourselves is always traced back to our own thoughts, emotions, and actions. So thinking, feeling, and acting in accordance with what we want will produce effects on the mental and spiritual planes that will then manifest the circumstances that bring what we want into our lives.

Interestingly, the authors of the *Kybalion* viewed the very discovery of the Hermetic Principles as such a circumstance in and of itself, since having this knowledge is what enables us to shape our own lives. As they write in the opening chapter, "...when the pupil is ready to receive the truth, then will this little book come to him or her. Such is The Law. The Hermetic Principle of Cause and Effect, in its aspect of The Law of Attraction, will bring lips and ear together—pupil and book in company." Perhaps the same could be said of your encounter with this guide!

Other Principles in the Hermetic system help complete the framework for how and why the Law of Attraction operates throughout every aspect of the Universe. In Part Two, we'll examine one that's particularly important to Witches—the **Principle of**

Mentalism, which states that the entire Universe is actually one giant "mind."

For now, however, it's worth acknowledging one element of the Law of Attraction that some people have a hard time accepting—what is often referred to as "the spiritual stuff."

The discomfort with such phrases as "the spiritual plane" or "the divine source" can be an obstacle for those with an atheist or agnostic worldview, as well as for those who practice a religion that doesn't align with the concepts presented in the *Kybalion* and other neo-Hermetic and New Thought texts.

This disconnect stems from two underlying thought processes. One is the idea that there's a strict division between science and spirituality, and that nothing that can't be proven through the scientific method should be taken seriously. The other is the association of words like "spiritual" and "divine" with the dominant monotheistic belief systems that center on a single deity, generally referred to as "God," who is responsible for all of creation, resides outside of our physical existence, and has the ability to reward or punish us based on our behavior.

But the philosophy underlying the Law of Attraction negates both of these ideas. For starters, the "God" of Hermeticism—a philosophy that predates monotheism—is envisioned as an all-encompassing force that is *within* our physical existence, and is co-creating the Universe along with us and everything else in it.

The *Kybalion* calls this co-creating force "The All" and offers this explanation of its non-separation from our actual selves: "While All is in THE ALL, it is equally true that THE ALL is in All." Other terms for this concept of divinity within Hermeticism include "The One," "The Creator," and "The Supreme Good."

However, even the word "divinity" is misleading, as it implies that there's a distinction between this "ALL" and mere mortals, when they are actually one and the same. Remember the Principle of Correspondence— "as above, so below." So whatever you want to call this force, it is present in every particle in the Universe. And as for the division we have been drawing between spirituality and science for the past few centuries, the skeptically-inclined are in luck: the two realms are starting to come together in unexpected and unprecedented ways.

THE QUANTUM CONNECTION

The past several decades have seen some astounding developments in the scientific fields known variously as quantum physics, quantum mechanics, and quantum theory.

With interesting parallels to the Hermetic tenets outlined in the *Kybalion*, the focus of this branch of physics has been a quest to understand the make-up and behavior of the Universe at the most basic level of reality—the subatomic level.

And while most quantum physicists will be quick to point out that they are dealing with theory, rather than proven phenomena, the similarities between the ancient wisdom and the modern ideas are too significant to ignore.

While a comprehensive look at the subject of quantum physics would fill several books, it's worth taking a look at a few elements in order to get a better sense of how the Law of Attraction is able to operate throughout the Universe.

Perhaps the most obvious connection is our modern understanding of the **Principle of Vibration**—thanks in no small part to Albert Einstein, who has been widely quoted as saying "everything is vibration."

Discoveries in quantum physics have led some scientists to describe the Universe as "vibrating strings of energy," and this is becoming more and more clear to researchers in the medical fields, who have found that different parts of the body have their own specific "sonic signature," vibrating at different rates from each other. In fact, there has even been some consensus that specific frequencies can repel and even destroy disease.

Of course, many professionals in the alternative healing arts are aware of the flip side of this phenomena: specific frequencies can also exacerbate or even cause disease, and this is an area where our thoughts—which also have frequencies—have particularly important impact.

So, remembering that like attracts like, it's always advisable to think as positively as possible, whether the subject is health or any other area of life.

As for the **Principle of Correspondence**, ever since the discovery of subatomic particles, it has become increasingly clear that the same fundamental structures make up everything in the Universe, whether it be living organisms, inorganic matter, or celestial bodies.

This seems to affirm the notion of "as above, so below; so below, as above" in more concrete terms than the ancient Greeks—who proposed the existence of atoms—might have ever expected.

What's more, scientists working with what is known as unified field theory (formerly known as the "theory of everything") have been developing an understanding that everything in the Universe is connected by a field of energy.

Another chief concept is Bell's theorem, which states that events happening from a distance can affect the rest of the Universe without any apparent direct energetic connection. Furthermore, David Bohm's "holonomic theory" suggests that each part of the Universe has the capacity to emulate the appearance and processes of the whole.

Again, these ideas are part of a much larger framework of theories about the nature of reality that is beyond the scope of this guide, but they serve here as just a few examples of how even the rational, evidence-based world of science is approaching the same conclusions the ancient sages came to thousands of years ago.

Perhaps the most exciting discovery, however, in relation to the Law of Attraction, is what has become known as "the observer effect."

Various experiments have shown that a photon will behave like a wave, rather than like a particle, when it is not observed by the human eye. Once it is observed, however, it pulls back into "focus" and appears as a particle.

Some quantum physicists have argued that this is essentially the nature of all reality—it is our observance of it that focuses the energy into what we are perceiving. This phenomenon relates to the Hermetic **Principle of Cause and Effect**, as well as to the workings of the Law of Attraction.

If our observation of reality has an influence on that reality, then it works to our advantage to focus our attention on the positive aspects of our experience, in order to bring about more of it!

While all of these concepts can be difficult, if not impossible, to wrap the mind around using any of your existing logic, it helps if you remember that our human perception of the Universe is extremely limited.

In fact, quantum physicists themselves have been baffled by many of their own discoveries, and this is partly why many of them would prefer that "New Age" writers and philosophers stop invoking these ideas in discussions of esoteric topics like the Law of Attraction. However, there are a few in the field who are more open to the notion that science may indeed be making its way back around to an inclusion of the spiritual.

Either way, there is really no need to understand one iota of quantum physics in order to put the Law of Attraction to work for you. As already stated in this guide, it's working in your life whether you're conscious of it or not.

MOVING FORWARD

Now that we've taken a brief tour of the physical (and metaphysical) underpinnings of the Law of Attraction, it's time to address some of the most common objections that skeptics raise when introduced to sources like *The Secret* and other teachings.

After all, unless you're already "magically inclined" as Witches are, or at least very open to truths that go beyond anything you've been taught in our skeptical mainstream culture, these ideas can be difficult to fully embrace.

If you have doubts, hopefully this next section will address at least some of them. Ultimately, however, there's only one way to truly prove that the Law of Attraction is real. You'll need to be willing to suspend your disbelief for long enough to try it out in your own life and witness your success.

DOUBT AND DISBELIEF: FREQUENTLY ASKED QUESTIONS

As you might expect, plenty of people who have encountered *The Secret* and/or other sources on the Law of Attraction have expressed criticisms about the message.

These range from arguments that only a small part of the overall picture is presented, which is a common view among Witches who write on the subject, to declarations that the whole thing is completely bogus.

In a sense, both of these statements are true.

The more mainstream sources do tend to just scratch the surface of how the Law of Attraction actually works, particularly when it comes to how to train the mind to consciously direct it.

And those who flatly reject any notion of some invisible force governing the circumstances of our lives will, like everyone else, always experience what they believe to be true, which means they will be unable to recognize any evidence of the Law of Attraction in their own lives.

But even believers experience obstacles, doubts, and difficulties in understanding just how it can be that every aspect of their life experience is created by their thoughts. Here we'll briefly address a few common concerns expressed by skeptics and practitioners alike.

Everyone knows that success is achieved through hard work. How is sitting around daydreaming about a better life going to change anything for me?

First, no one is suggesting you quit your job and devote yourself full-time to closing your eyes and visualizing your success. After all, in your current life, you probably still need to work to pay the bills.

But the equation of "hard work" with "success" is really a cultural myth that can do more harm than good. After all, plenty of people work very, very hard and can't get ahead no matter what they do, while others find immediate success with what feels like very little effort.

If you're focused on the idea that work should be hard, your work will always feel difficult to you, and success will always seem like a destination you haven't reached yet. But if you go about your work while keeping a positive frame of mind, not only does the work become easier, but you will also be more receptive to ideas, tips, and opportunities that can lead you to the promotion, new job, or other "lucky break" that will bring you the success that is currently eluding you.

If thoughts become things, why can't I make a monkey ride a bicycle into my living room right now?

The answer here has to do with probability, which is often left out of the discussion when it comes to the Hermetic Principles and/or quantum physics.

On the mental plane, if you are imagining a bike-riding monkey in your living room, you are indeed creating this scenario. However, on the physical plane, many factors have to be navigated before any idea can be made into reality. These include linear time, geography, and the existing circumstances of all the people, places, and things that would be involved.

In other words, our ideas can run into a lot of interference on their way to physical manifestation—including, and especially, our own doubts. So unless you happen to know a circus trainer who can bring a monkey and a bicycle over to your house, there's a very small probability that these circumstances will come together on the physical plane.

And *knowing* that the probability is small, you're automatically reducing the chances even further by projecting your doubt—however reasonable it may be—into the Universe.

Nonetheless, if you *really* have a strong desire to make this happen, it is possible. But it would likely require a lot of legwork on your part, and most people find that they'd rather develop their Law of Attraction skills for what they feel are more beneficial, as well as more probable, goals.

How am I supposed to think positively about my living situation when I hate it and desperately want to move?

Although this tends to be difficult to hear at first, the answer is to do your best not to think about it. The more you notice and actively focus on what you don't want, the more persistently it shows up in your life.

This is where appreciation can be a big help—find whatever you can identify as the good in the situation, no matter how seemingly small, and see how many aspects you can add to that list.

Whenever you start to dwell on the negatives, try to direct your attention to that list. If that seems impossible, gently allow yourself to think about other aspects of your life that are going well, until you notice that you're feeling better. And when you think about moving, imagine your ideal situation and how you will feel once you're in it.

If I create my reality, why in the world would I have chosen the terrible things that have happened to me?

This is often the hardest aspect of the Law of Attraction for people to wrap their minds around.

Most of the time, we're only unconsciously creating our reality. We're not deliberately choosing our thoughts, and we're unaware of all the activity going on in the subconscious mind.

So no, you are not deliberately choosing to attract negative circumstances. But your thoughts, whether they are conscious or unconscious, are creating your dominant vibrational frequency, which is attracting experiences that match it on a vibrational level.

These experiences may not match any *specific* thoughts that you've had in the past, but they do match up with some part of your dominant vibration. The good news is that as you learn to work with the Law of Attraction, you can raise your vibration to attract positive experiences, instead.

And there's no need to indulge in regrets about the past, or about your role in creating it. We can't undo the past—the only point of power is in the present, and in believing that your future will be better.

I think about what I want all the time, but it's still not here. What am I doing wrong?

There are two parts to this answer.

As explained above, everything that we're trying to draw to us has to contend with time and physical space, as well as the vibrational frequencies of any and all people who may be part of the equation. So it can feel like the thing we want isn't happening, when really it's just not manifesting according to our preferred timeline.

The problem we run into, then, is the second part— we end up focusing on the fact that it hasn't happened yet, which only brings us more of it *not* happening. In fact, often when we think about what we want, we're simultaneously thinking about the lack of it.

The trick is to focus on the belief that it will come to us, imagine how we will feel when it does, and *ignore* the fact that we don't have it yet. If we can practice this patience for long enough, and trust that what we want is coming, it will eventually come. It has to, because the Law of Attraction is universal and all-encompassing.

Things started to improve for me after I discovered how to work the Law of Attraction, but now everything is back to normal. What happened?

This is common.

People who really grasp the concept often get a significant vibrational "boost" just from the excitement of being liberated from their habitual thought patterns as they practice the art of deliberately choosing where to put their focus. This will often move a few positive things into place in a relatively short time. Maybe you get a surprise check in the mail, or you find that your days are going more smoothly, and you feel better about life in general.

You may sustain this higher vibrational state for several days, weeks, or even months. However, life will always bring us challenges, and if you were operating on a low or mixed frequency—which is the case for most people, there will be unwanted circumstances and experiences that have been making their way toward you for a long time.

Furthermore, the collective force of your old habitual ways of thinking has a very strong vibration that is easy to fall back into, particularly when you experience a challenge. In other words, old habits are hard to break, and new ones are hard to establish.

So don't be discouraged if you find you can't constantly sustain the positive frame of mind that you know has worked for you before. Just like learning to play an instrument or a new sport, working with the Law of Attraction takes practice, and even once you really start to master it, there will always be room for improvement.

PUTTING IT INTO PRACTICE

So far, we've introduced the basics of the Law of Attraction, taken a brief historical tour of both modern and ancient writings on the topic, and looked at discoveries in contemporary science that offer glimpses of how it is physically at work in our lives. By now, it's probably pretty clear to you that there's more to it than the phrase "like attracts like" would imply.

Indeed, making this principle work for you requires practice, patience, and the ability to understand that what we are able to perceive with our physical senses is only the tip of the iceberg when it comes to the vastness of the Universe. It also requires a willingness to work with, and trust, the unseen world—whether you call it the spiritual plane or something else.

If you investigate all the available resources on the Law of Attraction, you will no doubt find a plethora of different approaches and methods for tapping into the power of your own mind to direct the energies that shape your life. In Part Two, we'll examine how practitioners of Witchcraft, who have been working with these forces in a variety of ways for centuries, incorporate the Law of Attraction into their magical work.

You do not have to be a practicing Witch to find this information useful. However, if you've ever been curious about magic and spellwork, you may find that exploring it in the context of the Law of Attraction is just the doorway you've been looking for.

PART TWO

WITCHCRAFT AND THE MAGIC OF INTENTION

A TIME-HONORED TRADITION

Despite a long history of attempts to discredit, repress, and even eradicate it, the practice of Witchcraft remains very much alive and well today. In fact, given the growing popularity over the past few decades of Wicca—a religion with roots in Witchcraft—it could be argued that the Craft, as it is often referred to, is on the rise.

But what is Witchcraft, exactly? And what does it have to do with the Law of Attraction? Let's take a brief look at the connections between these two fascinating topics, and then examine in more detail how practitioners of the Craft work directly with the Law of Attraction to manifest desired changes in their lives.

"Witchcraft" is really an umbrella term for many different kinds of spiritual traditions that are focused on the natural world. The range of beliefs and practices that coexist under this umbrella is quite diverse.

For example, some people believe in and worship one or more deities, while others are strict atheists. Some participate in groups, as with covens and circles, while many are solitary practitioners. A full discussion of all these differences is ultimately beyond the scope of this guide. However, it's reasonably accurate to say that those who identify as Witches have a deep love and respect for the Earth and all of Nature, are individualistic and not inclined to "follow the crowd," and believe that they have the power to shape their own lives.

These days, the most widely known form of the Craft is Wicca, which was initially developed in England in the first half of the 20th century and later spread to North America and many other parts of the world.

As a religion, Wicca is centered on the worship of a pair of deities—the Goddess and the God—who are responsible for all of creation and who can be appealed to directly for assistance in all manner of challenges and desires. Like others who follow the path of the Craft, Wiccans strive to be in tune with the energies of Nature and see themselves as participants in creation, rather than just bystanders in a world that is happening around them.

The explosion of interest in Wicca over the past few decades has led to increased awareness of other forms of the Craft, and has even given rise to new, highly eclectic forms that may incorporate some Wiccan beliefs and practices but do not necessarily identify as Wiccan.

This uptick has also resulted in an explosion of resources—books, magazines, blogs and the like—for those interested in exploring the Craft. Many of these sources will mention the Law of Attraction. Some view it from a specifically Wiccan perspective, while others are less "denominational" in their approach. But no matter what form of Witchcraft any given author practices, when it comes to the Law of Attraction, the discussion will invariably be about the practice of magic.

So what is magic, then? In the context of Witchcraft, it's a term for the art of directly manipulating the natural energetic forces that shape our lives. It is practiced by Witches, including many (but not all) Wiccans, as well as others who follow various Pagan traditions but do not identify as Witches.

Magic takes many forms, and usually involves working with physical tools and ingredients, such as candles, crystals, and herbs, but it can also be performed with the body through ritual movement, chanting, and dance.

For example, some Witches might magically charge a piece of amber or amethyst for a happy day and then carry it in their pocket to ward off unwanted energy from negative coworkers. Others make "poppets" filled with specific herbs to draw money or a love relationship into their lives.

Weather magic may involve ritually sprinkling water onto soil to bring needed rain. Special teas brewed with healing herbs, in conjunction with spoken incantations or a ritual bath, can do wonders for curing a host of ailments. Drumming and dancing—two forms of magic practiced around the globe—are excellent ways to build positive energy that can be applied to any magical goal.

As you can probably see by now, the possibilities for utilizing magic, whether you're following a spell passed down through the generations or inventing one of your own, are truly endless!

APPLYING THE LAW OF ATTRACTION THROUGH SPELLWORK

Of course, as many experienced Witches know, magic can also be worked using nothing but the focused mind.

This last approach can be quite difficult—even impossible—for most beginners, so working with tools of some kind is considered the best way to start. Below, we'll offer a very simple magical working that anyone can use to practice focusing their attention on a specific goal.

But first, let's take a closer look at the philosophy behind the Law of Attraction, through the perspective of those who use magic to deliberately co-create their lives with the mysterious forces at work in the Universe.

HERMETICISM REVISITED

Many Witches have benefited from studying the Hermetic principles and understanding how to apply them to their practice of magic. In Part One we introduced three of the seven Hermetic principles as they form the larger framework in which the Law of Attraction operates: the Principles of Correspondence, Vibration, and Cause and Effect.

However, it's arguable that the first of these tenets is actually the most important one to understand from a Witch's perspective, and perhaps the most important in terms of the Law of Attraction as well: the **Principle of Mentalism**.

The *Kybalion* states that "the ALL is Mind; the Universe is Mental." Essentially, the fundamental make-up of the Universe is consciousness, or, as it has been understood in more modern times, information.

Another way to say this is that the Universe is one infinite mind, within which all things are possible. This is another concept that is often difficult for most people to grasp, but it starts to make more sense when you realize that nothing can materialize in the physical world without someone first imagining it. All inventions, whether they be technological or artistic, begin in the mind. Hermeticism takes this observation further with the assertion that all naturally-occurring phenomena also originated in the *divine* mind.

Interestingly, the Principle of Mentalism would seem to be the basis for creation myths from around the world, whether it's the biblical story found in Genesis, or the many stories from other religious traditions in which the world began with an *idea* on the part of the original creator.

Yet another way to look at it is through the lens of the unified field theory mentioned in Part One. The field of energy that connects everything in the Universe is actually consciousness, and it is through this interconnectedness that thoughts eventually become things.

Witches and other practitioners of magic know that when they focus their intentions for a specific outcome, they are using the mental plane to connect the energy of their individual minds with that of the Universal mind. This creates a conduit for the manifestation of their desires to flow from the spiritual plane into their physical experience.

When we remember the other components of the Hermetic system, we can further see how the process of manifestation works. Because of the Principle of Correspondence—"as above, so below"—the magical intention must become manifest on the spiritual plane.

Because of the Principle of Vibration, that intention is vibrating at a specific frequency. Now, provided that the sender of the intention has a dominant vibration that matches that frequency, the Law of Attraction will bring circumstances into the sender's experience that allow the manifestation to take place!

And though the result will often certainly feel like "magic," we know from the Principle of Cause and Effect that it is really just the effect caused by the sending of the intention.

There are three more Hermetic Principles that help to complete the picture of how the Universe operates, and how magic can be utilized to direct these forces. These are known as the Principles of Polarity, Rhythm, and Gender. For those inclined to study Hermeticism further, these tenets are well worth exploring. However, for our purposes, they are less relevant, as they apply to a more advanced understanding of magic than is necessary for our purposes.

Since our focus is on the role of the Law of Attraction in effective magic, let's turn now to a specific example of a magical working, with an eye toward how the concepts we've been discussing are applied in a practical way.

PRACTICAL MAGIC: A CANDLE SPELL FOR A MONEY BOOST

Candle magic—using the power of the element of fire to send an intention into the Universe—is a form that many beginners find success with rather quickly.

This simple spell, when performed with genuinely focused intention, can bring results in delightfully surprising ways.

The trick is to avoid trying to figure out *how* the extra money will show up in your life. When you focus on the "how," you're really signaling to the Universe that you don't trust it to work for you.

Consequently, the Law of Attraction will bring you more doubt, rather than more cash! Let's first review the instructions for the spell, and then we'll break it down into its components to see how the Law of Attraction is being applied each step of the way.

Instructions:

All you need is a small green or gold candle and a pin or paperclip. You can find spell candles (also sometimes called ritual or "mini" candles) in most New Age shops, but a votive will also do.

Be sure you have a candle holder or fire-proof plate to set the candle on.

Choose a calm and pleasant place where you'll be undisturbed, and be sure you can leave the candle to burn all the way down on its own (if you need to go to bed before it's spent, you can place it in a sink to finish burning).

Start by calming and grounding yourself. Listen to some soothing music and take long, slow, deep breaths.

Hold the candle between your palms, and visualize your personal power flowing into it, saturating the candle from the base to the top of the wick. This is called charging, and it's a crucial step in the process of magical manifestation.

If you like, you can speak your intention out loud, by saying:

"I now charge this candle with my personal power, to manifest new wealth in my life."

Now, spend a few minutes imagining the feeling of receiving money unexpectedly. Perhaps you can recall a time when you found a dollar on the ground or got a surprise check in the mail. If you can't recall any specific event, invent one.

Summon that feeling of happy surprise, and hold onto it for several moments as you visualize a pile of money appearing in your hands.

When you feel ready, use the pin (or one end of the paperclip) to carve a dollar sign ($) into the candle.

Then place it in its holder, and say the following words aloud:

> *"With this fire I summon Nature's forces,*
> *Money now flows to me from hidden sources."*

Light the candle, and as the wick catches, say *"So let it be."*

****

Before we look at each step of this simple spell, let's revisit the definition of magic that was offered above: the art of directly manipulating the natural energetic forces that shape our lives. While this is a useful definition, it doesn't get at *how* the manipulation of these forces is achieved.

Depending on who you ask, you will no doubt get different explanations for the "how," but most practitioners will probably agree that all magic boils down to *creating a vision* of what you want to achieve, and *powering it with the feeling of having achieved it.* Doing so effectively will then create and deliver circumstances into your life that match that vision and feeling.

Whether the results appear to be an exact match, a partial match, or even better than what you envisioned will depend on your ability to focus your energy and to trust in the outcome.

Each component of the spell is designed to maximize that focused energy.

THE INGREDIENTS

The first thing we notice about this spell is that it calls for specific ingredients—a candle and a tool for inscribing the symbol.

Human beings are physical creatures who spend their lifetimes creating, acquiring, and using physical objects as a fundamental aspect of everyday existence. Therefore, it makes sense that doing some kind of physical work as a component of magic helps us focus our mental energy on the desired outcome in a way that just dreaming about it may not be able to achieve. Tools provide us with a concrete way to send our specific message to the Universe about what we desire, and the enactment of the spell is the vehicle that sends that message.

Candles are very effective tools for beginners for several reasons. A candle is a physical representation of the element of fire, and therefore symbolizes transformation. You can see this as you watch the flame change the shape of the candle by melting the wax.

Candle magic is also highly interactive—you ignite the flame yourself, making something happen on the physical plane as well as the mental and spiritual planes. And then there's the nature of fire itself, which is just rather naturally magical and mesmerizing, provided you don't let it get out of control!

The color specification is also important. This is because magic in the Wiccan traditions often draws on a system of symbolic correspondences between spell ingredients and the purpose at hand. For example, every herb used in magic is associated with specific qualities and has universally recognized uses for particular magical aims: lavender is used to promote peace and relaxation, among many other goals, and chicory root is known to help overcome obstacles to achieving one's desires in life.

There can be several reasons for why a particular association is made, but underlying all correspondences is the Principle of Vibration. In other words, the vibrational frequency of lavender matches the frequency of calm and relaxation.

For beginners, correspondence is probably most easily understood when it comes to color. For example, red and pink are often associated with love, and it has been shown that these colors resonate with vibrations in the physical body that are associated with loving feelings. Orange and yellow can brighten one's mood, while blue and purple can have a calming effect.

This is all because colors are essentially light moving at different rates of vibration. The use of color is especially emphasized in candle magic, with every imaginable goal having one or more corresponding colors.

Green is associated with abundance due to its association with the vegetation we all rely on for survival, and is considered a color of fertility and new beginnings. Of course, it's an added bonus that green is the color of American money. Gold is universally associated with wealth and success, as is the precious mineral that bears its name! Both of these colors can lend strength to the signal you're broadcasting to the Universe in your request for extra money to come into your life.

As for the dollar sign, the use of symbols in magic is truly a long-standing tradition, as we can see in the ancient civilizations of the Egyptians, the Celts, and many other peoples around the globe. Symbols are a method of communication that transcends language, both on a mundane level, such as those used in traffic signs, and on the spiritual level, where the symbol itself is communicating with the divine mind.

There's a very wide range of possibilities for using symbols in magic. Many Witches particularly like to work with runes, letters of the ancient Celtic Ogham alphabet, astrological signs, and other systems of symbology that help them represent the specific outcomes they wish to attract. Symbols may be inscribed on magical tools, pendants and other jewelry, or drawn in the air as part of a ritual.

The use of the dollar sign inscription in this spell reinforces your message, in no uncertain terms, that you wish to attract money to you. As the symbol is transmuted into air via the melting of the wax, its message is received on the spiritual plane, where it will be answered with its likeness in the form of actual dollars.

Finally, you'll notice that the instructions include "charging" the candle before you enact the spell. This is an important step in all spellwork, and there are numerous methods for charging magical objects of all kinds. Some people charge their ingredients well ahead of time, while others do it as part of the specific working, as this spell calls for. Since it is your personal energy, or vibration, that is ultimately activating the magical manifestation, you want to be sure that you are directing that energy into the candle itself.

THE PHYSICAL AND MENTAL ENVIRONMENT

The spell recommends choosing a calm and pleasant place where you'll be undisturbed.

Just as you need a space to chop vegetables to prepare a meal, or a desk and a reasonable amount of quiet for writing or studying, it's important to have a designated environment for working magic. Most Witches have an altar or other work space where all of their spellwork takes place.

This can be a "dual-purpose" space if need be, such as a coffee table or dresser top, but for the spellwork to have maximum effect, it should be cleared of all mundane objects so that the focus of the space is clearly on your present task. You may also want to arrange the space with objects that are pleasing and/or related to the purpose for the magic. For example, you might include flowers, crystals, or images that make you think of abundance and wealth.

But it's not just the physical environment that needs tending to. Similarly, your mind needs to be a conducive environment for magical work.

If you are mulling over the events of your day, or your to-do list for tomorrow, or an ongoing problem you're still trying to solve, then you are not going to be sufficiently focused on your intention for the spell to be effective.

Calming the mind before working magic is essential. The suggestions presented here are just a few basic ways to get into the right "head space" for your task, but every mind is unique, and some methods for grounding and centering will work better than others, depending on who you are.

As we'll discuss later on, a regular practice of meditation can be incredibly helpful in reducing mental distractions, which benefits you not just in terms of magical work, but in every area of your life.

But no matter what your method may be, clearing away the clutter of the mind prepares your mental environment for the most important element of the work: visualization. This is true whether you're using magic or some other method for working with the Law of Attraction. The clearer your vision of what you want to bring into your life, the more effective your work will be.

THE VISUALIZATION

This component of the spell involves first summoning one or more memories that can start to activate the feeling of receiving an unexpected sum of money, whatever amount it may have been.

It then provides an option for inventing such an experience in your mind's eye—similar to the act of daydreaming. This process gets you closer to the optimal emotional state for attracting a new experience that matches what you are imagining.

You are then encouraged to combine that feeling with the image of your hands filling with money, and to hold that combination of thought and feeling until it feels real to you.

You are now creating an image on the mental plane, which you will send to the spiritual plane. It is with this positive energy that you will then carve the dollar sign into the candle and light the wick, sending the image with deliberate, focused intent.

You may have noticed that the amount of money you're visualizing is not specified in the spell. This is because it's usually easier to hold the belief that you will receive *some* money than it is to believe in a specific amount. It also helps you avoid discounting any manifestations if they don't equal the amount you have in mind.

Although it's certainly possible to intend for a specific amount and then receive individual increments that will ultimately add up to that amount, this is introducing more complexity into the magic than is useful for this beginner's experiment. As you become more adept at magic, you may want to try spells that are geared toward manifesting money more specifically.

THE WORDS

Most, but not all, spellwork involves spoken words of some kind. Language is a powerful tool, and spoken aloud, it creates a place where the mind and body join as one to communicate an intention deliberately to the Universe.

Like thoughts, words have their own vibrational frequencies, and just as they can be used to elicit strong responses from people, they can be used to signal to the spiritual plane what it is we're placing our focus on—and therefore, what we will attract.

Traditionally, spells have used rhythm and rhyme for two reasons. First, it makes spells easier to remember, which was handy for passing them down in the days when literacy levels were low and paper and ink were scarce. Second, the sound of the rhythm and rhyme can add a boost to the overall energy of the spell.

However, not all practitioners of magic use rhyme, as they find the "sing-songy" quality to be distracting. Instead, many will tailor the language of a pre-written spell to suit their own sensibilities.

This is an important element of spellwork: you have to believe the words you're saying, and be able to say them with focused intention.

If you're saying them mindlessly or doubtfully, the magic won't work. This is because, for all the power that words can have, the Universe actually responds to your feelings—your dominant vibration—rather than the words themselves.

THE RELEASE OF THE SPELL

The final step of the spell after lighting the candle is to say the words "so let it be."

This is one traditional way of "releasing" the work into the spiritual planes. It is also known as "sealing" the spell, and can be thought of as akin to sealing an envelope before putting it in the mailbox.

Different magical traditions may use different words for this step, but the purpose is essentially the same: to acknowledge that the work is done and send it on its way, and to help the practitioner transition back to the "ordinary" world, letting go of the focus on the spell's purpose, and trusting that it will be successful.

This last part is essential: trust that you *will* receive a surprise influx of money, without any further effort on your part. Remember, if you go around doubting the magic, Law of Attraction will simply bring you more reasons to doubt it.

After working this type of spell, many people like to sit and gaze at the candle flame for a few minutes, relaxing in the soft glow of the light. This is a great way to wind down after focusing so intently on your goal.

You will most likely notice a lighter, easier mood after working a candle spell. If this is the case, enjoy it! Any time your vibrational frequency is raised, do your best to run with it and keep it that way for as long as possible.

THREE CORE METHODS REVISITED

As discussed in Part One, among the plethora of sources on the Law of Attraction we find three essential approaches to making the Law work for you: appreciation, affirmation, and visualization. It's worth noting here that all three of these are at work in the spell above, and in much of magical practice in general.

Appreciation happens when you're recollecting past occurrences of receiving unexpected money, and summoning the positive feelings associated with those events. The same is true even if you're inventing these memories, because it's not about being factual. Rather, the task is to summon and hold the feeling of *appreciating* a positive experience around money.

This sense of appreciation should be at its height when you visualize the pile of money in your hands.

Remember, the Universe responds to your feelings, rather than your words.

Visualization, obviously, is the vehicle for summoning the necessary feeling of appreciation. The more vividly you can imagine the money in your hands—the look, feel, and even the smell of those bills—the stronger your positive vibration around the idea of receiving money becomes.

Notice that the visualization does not focus on *how* the money will arrive in your hands. That part is up to the Universe as it finds its own way(s) to respond to your request. All you need to do is visualize the end result. If you're trying to figure out how it will happen, you will undoubtedly close yourself off to the full scope of the possibilities, and end up limiting the potential for the spell to work

Affirmation, as defined in Part One, is "the act of repeating positive statements, whether silently or out loud, that describe the reality we're looking to create." This is where the spoken part of the spell comes in. By affirming that money flows to you from hidden sources, and that you are consciously directing the forces of Nature to make that happen, you strengthen the overall effect of the spell.

As you say these words, it's important to also actively feel *appreciation* for the results. The combination of this feeling and the spoken affirmation is what turns your intention for surprise money into a belief in it.

A common expression in the literature of Law of Attraction turns an old saying on its head: It's not "I'll believe it when I see it," but rather, "you'll see it when you believe it." Belief comes before manifestation, and affirmation, in the form of the spoken words of a spell, helps to create and strengthen the belief.

GOING FURTHER

So far, this guide has introduced the Law of Attraction as an underlying principle at work in the Universe that responds to your thoughts and emotions, bringing you circumstances that align with your dominant vibrational frequency. We have also examined the core principles of magic in light of how it works with the Law of Attraction to bring about desired change, and illustrated an example spell for you to try.

While it's true that all of these concepts are at the core of a profound framework for making unprecedented improvements in your life, it's also true that knowing is really only half the battle. After all, if we could all simply begin to think positively—and only positively—starting right this minute, wouldn't the world be a vastly different place?

The truth is, changing your thoughts is much easier said than done, especially if you're focused on areas of your current reality that you're not pleased with.

Practicing magic can certainly help create the shift you're striving for, but ultimately you'll also need to do some excavating of the buried layers of thought that are helping to create your current outlook.

Most of us are unaware of the underlying beliefs and ideas that cause resistance to changing our thoughts. Taking a closer look at what thought actually *is* and its impact on us can help us to release old thinking habits and develop new ones.

In Part Three, we'll examine the concept of *thought forms* and their role in the shaping of the circumstances of our lives. We'll offer a few practices for becoming more conscious directors of our own mental energy, as well as a few magical workings for dealing with thought forms, for those so inclined.

MAKING THE SHIFT FROM THOUGHTS TO THINGS

THOUGHT FORMS: THE BUILDING BLOCKS OF YOUR REALITY

The biggest challenge for everyone who seeks to work with the Law of Attraction is changing long-standing patterns of thought.

It can be very hard to form new beliefs about areas of your life that you find challenging, especially if you have a long history with unwanted experiences around them. And it can be more difficult the older you are, since you'll have built up your beliefs over a longer period of time and are more susceptible to rigid thinking. (Older people often say that young people are "too impressionable," but when it comes to the ability to form positive beliefs, this can really be an advantage!)

In fact, scientists who study the brain have discovered that repeated thought patterns actually wear deep grooves in neural pathways, making it increasingly easier for those same thoughts to travel through the mind over and over again. However, it's also possible to create new neural pathways with new thought patterns, and leave the old, unwanted thoughts to fade away over time.

So how do we consciously create new habits of thought, in order to attract the circumstances we desire into our lives? First, it helps to take a closer look at thought itself, and the effects that our own thoughts, and the thoughts of others, have on our daily experience.

As discussed in Part One, both modern science and ancient wisdom assert that all matter is vibrational energy, mental at its most basic level. If this is so, then thoughts, too, are vibrational energy. Thoughts take an actual form (invisible though it may be) due to a sort of "build-up" of mental energy which occurs through the thinker's repeated focus on the thought.

The concept of thought forms is believed to originate with ancient Tibetan mysticism, but is also found in many spiritual, psychological, and philosophical traditions, including Witchcraft and Western occult systems, as well as some contemporary literature on the Law of Attraction.

Of course, explanations of what a thought form actually is will vary from one tradition to the next. For example, some extend the meaning to include esoteric concepts like spirits and deities. For our purposes, we'll focus on a fairly narrow definition: activity that takes place in the conscious and subconscious mind. Let's start with examining the relationship between thoughts and beliefs.

Thoughts can be said to range in "size," (or, more accurately, strength) according to how much energy goes into them.

Trivial thoughts are unlikely to garner enough accumulated energy to take any lasting or substantial form. They are fleeting ideas that are only relevant to a very specific point in time, such as hearing the kettle whistle and recognizing that it's time to take the boiling water off the stove—you're not likely to think much about this action once you've made your tea.

More significant thoughts, on the other hand, are likely to be repeated, especially when they're about any number of the ongoing circumstances of your life, or an issue in the larger world that you're interested in or have strong opinions about. These are the thoughts that take form, and repeated over time, as they gain more and more energy, they eventually strengthen enough to become beliefs.

For example, if you're unhappy at your job and tend to brood about it even when you're not at work, you're likely creating a belief that the job will never become enjoyable, and that you can't be happy unless you leave it. If you're constantly paying attention to negative news in the media, you're creating and strengthening a belief that life is inherently difficult, unfair, or even tragic.

Beliefs are what shape our responses to everything that happens in our lives, for better or for worse.

If you believe, for example, that you live in a dangerous neighborhood, you're going to be unable to ever completely relax when you're at home. This kind of consistent tension, no matter how subtle, has an effect on your well-being. It creates a certain anxiety, and it keeps you isolated from what could be a beneficial acquaintance with one or more of your neighbors.

Then, if and when a crime occurs in your neighborhood, the incident will reinforce your belief that your home is in a dangerous place, which just increases your level of tension and isolation. And if others in your neighborhood have beliefs similar to yours, there's a greater likelihood that everyone will hide out from each other instead of banding together to strengthen the community.

The resulting atmosphere of distrust can actually attract *more* crime, since like attracts like, but even if the crime level stays consistent, the quality of life for the members of the community will be less than it could be, because of these thought forms that have solidified into beliefs.

Viewed in this light, you might say that thought forms are the building blocks of the human experience. They certainly influence your life more than you probably realize.

The good news is that once you gain an understanding of what thought forms are and how they work, you can really learn to use them to your advantage in your everyday life, building the ones that are beneficial and deconstructing and releasing those that aren't.

And as you learn to exert more control over your thoughts, you will attract more positive circumstances into your life. So let's take a closer look at these invisible, often subtle, yet crucial clusters of energy.

SOURCES OF THOUGHT FORMS AND THEIR IMPACT ON YOU

So where do thought forms come from? The first and most important source is, of course, you!

You create and sustain innumerable thought forms all by yourself as you go about your life. You may express these out loud to other people, or keep them to yourself. You are consciously aware of many of your thought forms, but you are unconscious, or at least only half-conscious, of plenty of them as well.

For example, the residents of the "dangerous" neighborhood described above are likely operating from both conscious and unconscious thought forms. The conscious thought forms keep them locking their doors at night, which, of course, is a reasonable practice to be in.

But there's likely an unconscious—or at least less conscious—thought form going on underneath that says "I can't trust the people in this neighborhood. I am alone here."

This is what keeps you, and others in the neighborhood, locked out of a true sense of community. Each resident who has their own version of the "danger" thought form will be reluctant to reach out to others.

The only way you can improve the situation is to decide not to give any more energy to thoughts that make you feel vulnerable or suspicious. Instead, begin to pay attention to the positive aspects of your neighborhood, however slight they may seem.

If you can succeed at this, your sense of comfort—and therefore your life—will improve. And if you stick with it, opening yourself to as many positive thought forms as possible, you will most likely find that there are friendly, trustworthy neighbors around, whom you just didn't notice when you were focusing your attention on the sense of danger.

The next source of thought forms is the people with whom you interact in your life—your family, friends, co-workers, etc. You hear others expressing their own thought forms all the time, such as when someone says "I've always got too much work to do," or "it's best not to get your hopes up."

These are beliefs that the people in your environment are strengthening within themselves by saying them out loud. You may or may not share their beliefs, but as long as the person speaking them believes them, then it's true for them in their own experience.

Often, it can be hard not to be affected by the spoken thought forms of the people around us. As a small child, you picked up all kinds of thought forms from your parents and/or other family members, as well as teachers and friends, about how the world works and about who you are. And you have most likely carried many of these thought forms with you, often subconsciously and completely unexamined, ever since.

As an adult, however, you have the ability to recognize a thought form that comes from someone else, and decide for yourself whether you agree with it. Now, the ultimate practice in gaining mastery over your thoughts will be to apply the same discernment to the thought forms in your own mind that you would apply to those expressed by others.

The final source of the thought forms that we interact with on a daily basis is the larger society we live in. These thought forms may be expressed by friends, families, and others in our immediate environment, but they are also broadcast across the culture—and indeed, the globe—via television, social media, and other technologies of the Information Age.

These can be trivial or significant, from cultural standards of beauty to political opinions to views about ethics or morality. Any given thought form may have varying degrees of influence on individual people; for example, the thought forms surrounding the phrase "climate change" can cause anything from extreme fear in some people to complete denial in others, with a range of levels of concern in between.

The influence that a broader thought form has on you depends on how it interacts with your own personal thought forms, both conscious and unconscious. But all cultural and societal thought forms are worth evaluating with the same level of scrutiny that you'd apply to those expressed by the people around you, and those coming from your own mind.

Which are useful, and which are merely distracting or discouraging? Which are truly worth paying attention to? These considerations matter, since every thought you allow into your focus, no matter the source, is shaping your life.

Indeed, the principle of "like attracts like" applies to thoughts as much as any other aspect of your experience. Negative thoughts attract more negative thoughts, and the longer you stay focused on them, the more you attract, until your dominant vibrational frequency is one that is not conducive to bringing in positive thoughts or circumstances.

Anyone who has spent a lot of time watching or reading the news has almost certainly experienced a palpable drop in their mood, due to the mainstream media's near-exclusive focus on misfortune and tragedy. So be mindful of where you place your attention, and seek out upbeat, inspiring media, whether it be books, movies, or anything else that puts you in a positive frame of mind.

UNEXPRESSED THOUGHT FORMS

For the most part, whether they originate with you, are communicated by others in your environment, or are broadcast by society at large, the thought forms that truly impact you are playing out inside your own mind.

These are the thoughts that feed into your inner monologue, the conscious part of you that is reacting to the circumstances you find yourself in, that worries about the future or regrets the past, etc.

Your inner monologue has a great deal to do with the vibrational frequency you're sending out into the Universe, and consequently with what you attract into your life. It is this stream of thought that you will find yourself noticing more and adjusting more consciously as you begin to practice working with the Law of Attraction.

It's worth noting, however, that thought forms *external* to your own mind can also impact you, especially if you're a sensitive type.

Remember, thought is energy in its own right, and it doesn't have to be coming from within or verbally expressed by another in order to be perceived. This happens most often with emotions, which are an essential component of thought forms (indeed, most of our thoughts are accompanied by one or more emotions) and can be easily transferred from one person to another.

For example, if you're even remotely empathic, and someone near you is very angry or frustrated, you'll likely sense their emotions, even if the other person isn't outwardly expressing them. When we feel the emotions of others, they can easily affect our own inner monologue, for better or for worse.

What's more, if you're particularly sensitive, you can also experience thought forms that have nothing to do with anyone in your life.

You may be struck by a sudden sense of fear or sadness when walking past a place where a tragedy or disaster once occurred, even if you're unaware of the event. Particularly strong thought forms often hang around the physical places where they originated, long after their creators have left. (This is what gives many "haunted" places that "spooky" feeling.)

The only problem with this is when people assume the emotion they suddenly feel is their own, and then try to identify its cause. This can lead down a pathway of negative thought as we comb our lives for problems to focus on, re-energizing a negative inner monologue that was best left ignored!

So the next time you find yourself feeling an unpleasant emotion that seems to have no context in the moment, consider the possibility that it may not be coming from you.

Sometimes this alone is enough to clear away the clouds. But no matter what the source of negative feelings may be, resist the temptation to follow them down the old ruts of negativity in your mind. Focus on something else, instead, until you feel better.

LIMITING BELIEFS AND UNDERLYING EMOTIONS

When taking stock of their life circumstances, most people have at least one area that they feel content with, and at least one that seems perpetually lacking.

Likewise, some areas are easier than others when it comes to confidently visualizing positive improvements. You might feel great about your financial situation, but worry constantly about your health. Or you may be very optimistic about meeting someone new, but pessimistic about your career prospects.

The differences in our outlook between one area and another come from the differences in our thought forms around these subjects. When it comes to the part(s) of your life that you struggle with consistently, there are bound to be some well-entrenched thought forms holding you back.

Another term for these thought forms, used by psychologists, life coaches, and self-help authors, is "limiting beliefs." These beliefs, which keep us locked out of our true potential, can be so ingrained in us that we don't even know they're there.

Whether conscious or unconscious, limiting beliefs have their roots in thoughts that were formed in response to an experience. For example, people who really struggled academically in school may come to believe they're not as intelligent or even as hard-working as others, even though their challenges may have stemmed from factors that were completely unrelated to their intellectual capabilities—such as the quality of their home life, differences in learning styles, or a mismatch between teacher and student.

This limiting belief about their abilities often goes unchallenged throughout the rest of their lives, keeping them from even *considering* pursuing a higher level of education that could open up new opportunities.

In addition to personal experiences, lifelong exposure to cultural and societal beliefs can also keep us from being open to positive change.

For example, you may have a hard time truly believing that you could ever be as wealthy as you want to be. Perhaps you work in a field that doesn't pay well and most likely never will. Being a reasonable person, you probably also have a healthy appreciation for the odds of winning big in the lottery, even if you do occasionally buy a ticket. And as far as you know, none of your relatives is going to be leaving you a significant inheritance when they pass on.

If these or similar thoughts crop up whenever you think about your financial prospects, then you're operating from limiting beliefs, and keeping the abundance you crave out of your life. This may seem counter-intuitive—after all, things like your salary and the odds of the lottery are clear, verifiable facts, and what does "belief" have to do with facts?

The limiting belief is that your salary, the lottery, or inheritance are the *only* possible sources of significant abundance that could possibly manifest in your life. In reality, money can manifest in a million different unexpected ways, but as a culture we tend only to see a few possible avenues.

This is reinforced every time you or someone around you says "if only I could win the lottery, all my problems would be solved!" This thought form is literally saying that winning the lottery is the *only* way to true fortune!

Indeed, we live in a fairly pessimistic culture when it comes to money. While we recognize that some people who work hard can end up with plenty of wealth, we also know that for the majority of people, hard work does not obtain this result, no matter how deserved it may be.

Furthermore, there's a cultural value placed on being "realistic" when it comes to money. It's okay to daydream about winning the lottery, and many a pleasant conversation has been had about such fantasies, but there's an unspoken agreement—or thought form—that accepting your lot in life is the sensible thing to do.

No matter what area of life you'd like to improve, the bottom line is that if you think you need to be able to see *how* your goals are going to manifest, you're operating from the limiting belief that there are *no possibilities* beyond what you can see. And since the Universe brings to you what you project out into it, you will continue to not manifest your goals, until you learn to be truly open to the unexpected.

But you may have to do some deeper digging before you can really trust your ability to manifest circumstances that are different from what you've experienced before. Often, in order to release a limiting belief, you also have to address the emotions that accompany these limiting thought forms.

It turns out that money is a tough area of manifestation for a lot of people, due both to the kinds of limiting beliefs described above and to underlying emotions surrounding the idea of money.

Many people suffer from what has been called "poverty consciousness" or a "scarcity mindset," always perceiving matters of money and abundance in terms of there never being enough. This can be a constant cause of fear and misery, which is obviously not going to attract positive experiences pertaining to money.

Other people may feel a sense of guilt for wanting more than they have, making it hard to put completely sincere energy into attempts to manifest more. This can be quite common among people who identify as "spiritual" types, who then allow their lack of financial abundance to reinforce the sense that they should focus on other, more important aspects of life.

Indeed, consciously deciding that money doesn't matter can make it easier to deal with the feeling of not having enough of it. But if you keep feeding your negative thought forms around money, they will continue to keep it out of your life!

Love and relationships are another key area that some people struggle with more than others. Again, one's emotional state when thinking about love is key to manifesting it.

You're not likely to have much luck attracting a new partner the day after a breakup with someone you were attached to, for example, because whatever sadness, anger, and/or other negative emotions are involved in the breakup will be very strongly influencing your vibrational frequency. People in this situation need to take some time to heal before they can become vibrationally capable of attracting a new, joyful relationship into their lives.

There can be other hidden vibrational frequencies as well, such as a lack of self-love or a fear of abandonment, that keep lasting love from manifesting.

Finally, there can be the same barrier of "practicality" that so many people face around money. If you don't see definite possibilities for meeting new people in your daily life, you may decide that you never will.

On the other hand, there are people who find that love is far easier than money when it comes to deliberate manifestation. This could be due to the fact that on the whole, the concept of "love" is surrounded by far more positive thought forms than negative ones.

For example, unlike money, love is never referred to as "the root of all evil." In fact, it is seen as existing outside the influence of money or greed. It could also be argued that love just seems to be more associated with *magic*, arriving, as it often seems to do, "out of the blue."

Indeed, even though we may not be able to imagine where our next relationship will come from any more clearly than we can see the possible avenues for more wealth to come in, some people are just not as hindered by their blindness to the future when it comes to love. It really all depends on what your life experiences have led you to expect, and the thought forms you've been carrying around about the possibilities for love in your life.

STRATEGIES FOR RAISING YOUR FREQUENCY

You may or may not share the beliefs and feelings about love or money discussed above, but it should be clear by now that no matter which area of life you're working with, your own thoughts, beliefs and emotions are key to attracting what you desire.

So how can you change these seemingly ingrained habits of mind in order to change your life? You can start by simply getting into the habit of observing your thoughts.

The next time you find yourself feeling particularly happy or unhappy—no matter how subtle the feeling may be—stop, step back, and ask yourself what it is you've been thinking that has generated this emotion. There may be several thoughts coexisting or following each other in rapid succession. Try to identify each one on its own, as much as you can.

Don't judge yourself or argue with yourself over whether or not the thought is "true." Just acknowledge the thought, and pay attention how the energy of it feels to you. All you're doing at this stage is observing the processes of your own mind, and recognizing the connection between thought and emotion.

This practice is easier to get into in calm moments than in the midst of a hectic day or a difficult emotional experience. Don't worry or get frustrated with yourself if you forget to watch your thinking for long stretches of time. But do be willing to adopt new habits and practices that will get you closer to a vibrational frequency that matches what you're seeking to attract into your life.

Next, we'll introduce three useful methods for making the necessary shift in your habits of thought: meditation, journaling, and expressing gratitude.

MEDITATION

If you're a reader of "New Age" spiritual or self-help books, including other sources on the Law of Attraction, you've surely encountered at least one author encouraging you to meditate regularly. This is because meditation is incredibly beneficial in numerous ways for your mind, body, and spirit.

On a practical level, it serves as a way of "resetting" the brain in a way that sleep cannot, for various reasons having to do with the complex biology of human beings. It allows for a quieting of the extraneous, nonessential energy running around in our minds, which often includes worry, anxiety, resentment, and other negative thoughts and emotions. It also helps clear space for effective visualization, which, again, is a core strategy for working with the Law of Attraction.

A practice of just 10 to 15 minutes a day, if followed over the course of a few weeks, will start to create a noticeable difference in how you respond to experiences that normally trigger bouts of upset or aggravation.

You'll find yourself more easily connecting with your intuition, and the ability to see your thoughts as separate from you—as *forms* of their own that do not have to be hanging around in your head if you don't want them there. Ultimately, you'll find yourself able to detach more easily from disturbing, stressful, or otherwise unpleasant thoughts, and make more space for neutral and (eventually) positive thoughts to take their place.

So, no matter how your personal meditation practice takes shape, make a commitment to slowing down your mind for a few minutes on a daily basis.

You can find a wide array of guided mediations online, which are particularly helpful for beginners. Don't worry about "doing it right," as there's truly no way to get it wrong.

Even if your meditation sessions are full of thoughts and other distractions at first, the effort you're making to quiet your mind is making a difference. Keep at it, and you'll soon notice that it's helping you to raise your vibrational frequency, and to begin attracting more positive experiences into your life.

JOURNALING

Another good way to decrease and release negative thoughts is to keep a journal and write in it regularly. Whether it's a fancy leather-bound, embossed journal or a plain old notebook, having a designated place to express yourself privately is a great way to examine your thought forms and make conscious decisions about whether they're serving you.

In fact, as you write, you're pretty much guaranteed to discover more of those underlying, unconscious thoughts that have been buried under the surface of your busy conscious mind. The insights you gain in this process can be invaluable for identifying and releasing thought forms that are blocking positive manifestation.

Keep in mind, however, that while it's good to examine and release negative thoughts and emotions, there's always a risk of moving from "venting" about your struggles into "dwelling."

Keep an eye out for this tendency. Remember that the goal is to identify sources of negative thinking, but not to reinforce that negativity.

It can be a fine line at times, so practice paying attention to how you're feeling—in other words, to your vibrational frequency—as you write. As you do so, you'll learn to detect that moment when you're shifting from the relief of expressing your concerns to the sinking feeling that comes with obsessing over what you're seeing as "the problem."

Once that feeling hits, it's time to shift gears. If you can, start evaluating the thought forms you've identified around the problem you're writing about. Take each idea individually and consider it as objectively as possible.

Ask yourself if the thought is really *true*. If the answer is yes, ask yourself whether it *has* to be true from now on. In other words, start dismantling the thought form and creating space for new, positive truths to come into your life.

Note: depending on the subject, you may or may not be ready for this step in the process. If this endeavor is making you feel worse rather than better, then it's time to put the pen down!

Of course, it's also an excellent idea to write about what's going well for you, and to focus on positive feelings and thought forms.

In fact, journaling is an opportunity to put appreciation and affirmation into practice. Try writing about everything that's going well in your life, and find positive affirmations that you can write over and over again, such as "everything is working out for me" and "all is right in my world."

Challenge yourself to write only positive statements for three pages, or 15 minutes, or whatever goal feels sufficiently challenging to you. Then, take note of the difference in how you feel and appreciate yourself for putting in the effort to raise your vibration!

PRACTICING GRATITUDE

Even if you decide that journaling is not for you, do be sure to develop a daily practice of gratitude, or appreciation.

One of the most powerful ways to shift your experience of daily life is to actively recognize and express appreciation for the things that are going well. Even in the most challenging of times, there are always many aspects of your life that can be viewed as blessings, no matter how much you may take them for granted.

Start getting in the habit of making a list—either mentally or in writing—of what you are grateful for on a daily basis. Aim for a minimum of 10 items every day.

These can be very basic, like having a roof over your head, a job, or food in the kitchen. They can range in relative significance, from a pleasant few moments during your morning commute to a promotion or the beginning of a new relationship.

You might make this a nightly ritual, just before you go to sleep, or perhaps first thing in the morning, to get your day started on the most positive note possible.

The importance of appreciation can't be overstated: no matter what's going on in your life, be sure to always acknowledge the positive. As you get more practiced, you'll see how easily the list expands, as your thought forms relating to "gratitude" grow stronger.

Remember, like attracts like, so the more you focus on the existing positive elements of your life, the more successful you'll be at manifesting even greater positive circumstances.

TRANSFORMATION AS A WAY OF LIFE

As you work with meditation, journaling, and practicing gratitude, you will start to have a much clearer awareness of which of your thoughts are serving you well and which are impeding your ability to manifest your desires.

This ability to observe your thought forms and limiting beliefs from a neutral place means you can actually choose which thoughts to focus on and leave the rest, just as if you were choosing the colors you'd use to create a painting.

The thought forms that don't serve you will become less and less powerful, eventually falling away as they are no longer fed with the energy that comes from your attention. Those that you choose to keep "feeding"—i.e., paying attention to—will grow stronger and become easier to access.

For example, when it comes to financial abundance, you can recognize and then release your sense of lack, or the false sense that money matters just can't get better for you. You can focus instead on what you do have, truly appreciate it, and summon the peaceful feeling of having all your needs met.

Now that your attention is focused on a positive feeling, you're better positioned to attract more abundance.

You will also, no doubt, come to understand that some of these negative thought forms are much more stubborn than others. Those limiting beliefs that have long held you back in certain areas of your life are energetically powerful and will not go away permanently without a deliberate choice to let them go, over and over again when need be.

This is why so many people give up on the idea of "positive thinking"—no matter how good it makes them feel for a little while, their negative thought forms seem to just keep coming back! Understand that this is ultimately a life-long process, and have patience with yourself. Know that you are making progress even when you can't see the evidence yet.

And remember that the Universe has its own timing, which often may not fit with your preferred timing, but which will ultimately bring to you what you're seeking to attract, provided you keep working to raise your vibration.

THOUGHT FORMS AND MAGIC

Of course, Witches and others who practice magic know that there are strategies we can put in place to raise our vibrational frequency to a level that allows what we desire to come into our lives. Through spellwork, we can intentionally release negative thought forms and even create positive ones to more deliberately manifest our intended outcomes.

We'll offer a few examples of such workings below, but first let's take another look at the practice of magic with this concept of thought forms in mind.

Once you accept that thought takes form, and that the more energy a thought form receives, the more powerful it becomes, then you can begin to see *spells themselves* as thought forms. Indeed, all magic can be viewed as the directed use of thought forms.

In this framework, successful "tried and true" magical methods are successful because they have been used many times by many different people over time—in some cases, for centuries. In other words, the repeated focus on a particular ritual, incantation, or set of ingredients has, over time, made it more and more powerful.

For example, consider the various systems of magical correspondences discussed in Part Two, some of which date back to ancient times.

It's likely that after any given correspondence—such as the magical properties of a plant or a color—was first observed or intuited, it was then tested, confirmed and communicated to other magical practitioners. In this way, through the passing on of magical lore, the thought form containing the knowledge of the correspondence spread and strengthened with each new instance of attention to it and use of it in magic.

So when we use the color red to manifest an experience involving passion, for example, we're drawing on the energy of centuries of years of experience, and connecting with that very powerful universal thought form on the spiritual plane.

However, the benefit of following traditions laid down by other magical practitioners is lost if you are not feeling comfortable and connected with the actions and words called for by the spell you're working. Some people struggle with fully "getting into" spells offered by others, no matter how credible the source.

For example, as mentioned in Part Two, if the words of a particular spell don't resonate with you, it will be hard to say them in a way that will "convince" the Universe that you truly desire the thing that you're affirming. In this case, it's best to adapt the spell in a way that feels most true to your own self, and/or create your own spells from scratch.

Of course, this is easier said than done if you're just starting out. If you're new to magic, you may need to try various kinds of spells to get a sense for what you're most comfortable with. As you gain experience, you can start using spells from sources you trust as templates for your own unique spells, until eventually you have your own particular style of magic, relying on your own tried and true thought forms to manifest the changes you desire in your life.

The following spells and rituals provide concrete methods for working with thought forms to achieve a better state of mind for working successfully with the Law of Attraction.

The first two offerings are aimed at clearing unwanted negativity and eliminating old, well-entrenched thought forms from your consciousness. These are fairly simple and can be performed by anyone at any level of experience with magic.

The third spell is somewhat more advanced, and requires more practice in meditation and visualization to be truly effective. If you're new to magic, you may want to work with more basic spells for a while before giving this one a try.

A SACRED CIRCLE
ENERGY CLEANSING

Thought forms are actually visible to some clairvoyant people, who can see them with their "third eye." This skill is often used in energy healing, where unwanted thought forms, which appear as dark or dingy "spots" on the aura, are detected and then removed from the affected person's energy field.

The visualization in this ritual draws on the same concept, but you do not have to be practiced at "seeing" auras to experience the benefits.

Doing this work within a circle of sea salt adds extra effectiveness—the salt's purifying qualities will enhance the clearing, while its protective qualities will seal out any stray or unwanted energy while the spell is underway. For even more powerful effects, try working this spell when the moon is waning.

Before you begin, it's best to take a ritual cleansing bath, which will give you an energetic "head start" on the clearing process. You can add sea salt, calming essential oils, and/or herbs to the bath to create a soothing transition from your everyday "reality" into a magical, healing mindset. (If you don't have a bathtub, a nice hot shower will also do the trick.)

You will need:

- 1 white candle
- 1 smudge stick and a bowl of soil or loose smudging herbs and a fire-proof dish (*Note: White sage is considered to be the best traditional herb for energetic clearing work, but you can also use Silver King Artemisia (a related plant), cedar, rosemary, or lavender.*)
- 1 feather (optional)
- Sea salt

Instructions:

After your ritual bath (or shower), gather your ingredients and place them in the center of what will be your circle, whether this is on your altar or the floor. Open a window (at least a crack) so the old, unwanted energy will have somewhere to go, rather than lingering around in your space.

Light the candle, then mark your circle with a solid line of salt, affirming as you do so that you're creating a sacred circle where only positive energy exists.

If you like, you can say *"All that is wanted stay in; All that is unwanted jump out,"* or similar words.

From the center of the circle, ignite the smudging herbs.

Use the feather or your dominant hand to wave the smoke all around your body, starting at your feet and moving upward. Be sure to fan the smoke behind yourself as well, so that you fully clear your energy field.

As you work, visualize your body filling with light, and repeat the following or similar words:

"As I stand in my full power, I send all negative energy out of my being and bring forth Universal light in its place."

If your third eye picks up any "dusty" or grey areas, visualize them leaving your body and dissolving as they float out the opened window.

Once you've reached the top of your head, keep going for about another foot.

When you're finished, allow the smudging herbs to smolder out on their own (if using a smudge stick, lay it gently in the bowl of soil).

Sweep up and discard the salt.

You should now feel calm, clear, and receptive to positive energy.

"STARVING" STUBBORN THOUGHT FORMS

For routing out more persistent negative thought forms—those which are usually self-created and highly disturbing or annoying—the most effective methods involve simply refusing to "feed" them with any more energy.

To do this, you need to introduce alternative thought forms and/or actions to focus on instead.

Here are a few possibilities to try whenever a negative thought or feeling sneaks up on you:

- Sweep your dominant hand across your forehead and "pull" the thought from your brain, then fling it far from your body. Visualize it flying out of the Earth's atmosphere and being obliterated by the heat of the Sun.

- Say to it in a cheerful voice, *"No thanks, not interested. Please transmute to light."* Imagine closing a door on it before it can enter your inner space.

- For particularly disturbing, fear-based thoughts, visualize a globe of golden light surrounding the thought and evaporating it. Say *"I neutralize this energy and transform it into love and light."*

You may have to repeat your chosen method several times over a long period of time, but eventually you will starve the thought form out of existence, just as an unwanted salesperson will eventually stop knocking on your unanswered door.

If something is particularly bothersome or interfering, you might consider consulting a professional energy healer who can help you speed things along.

A DIRECTED
THOUGHT FORM SPELL

Although the majority of what we call "thought forms" are largely unintentionally or unconsciously created, you can also *purposefully* create a thought form and send it forth into the Universe to achieve an intended aim.

The key is to be clear and specific in the creation of the thought form. It's a bit like programming a robot to complete a specific task for you—if you don't describe exactly what you need done, it may not get done correctly, or at all!

Be sure your mind is clear and calm—do not create and program a thought form when you're feeling actively anxious about achieving your aim, or your "assistant" will be confused by the negative energy you're putting into it, whether you mean to or not.

If you just can't seem to clear your mind, try meditating for at least 15 minutes before working the spell. Incense or essential oil in a diffuser can also be very helpful for shifting into the necessary psychic state. For incense, you might try frankincense, patchouli, or nag champa. Essential oils of cinnamon, lavender, or sandalwood are also good choices, but in either case, go with what works best for you.

One important thing to note about intentionally created thought forms is that they will not simply "disappear" on their own completely, even if you forget about them. That's why it's recommended that you instruct the thought form to dissolve either when the manifestation has occurred, or after a specified amount of time passes.

Many Witches recommend no longer than 7 days, as eventually the thought form can lose its focus and/or collect energetic "dust," complicating or even thwarting your results.

(*Note:* if you don't see results within 7 days, don't automatically assume your spell didn't work. It may be that it simply takes longer for the results to manifest in your experience, so you might want to give it a bit more time before trying again.)

You will need:

- Incense (or essential oil) of your choice
- 1 white spell candle (or color associated with your specific aim)
- Paper and pen for working out your exact instructions

Instructions:

Sit comfortably in a quiet place where you will not be disturbed. If you incorporate circle-casting into your practice, do so before sitting down.

Spend some time thinking about your goal, and visualizing what your life will look and feel like once it has been met. It can be helpful to do some free-writing about this, especially if it's something you have strong emotions about.

Once you feel you have a solid sense of what you want to achieve, write it down in a clear, simple sentence in the form of a command. For example, you can say "Manifest the arrival of my next romantic interest."

Light the candle and center yourself.

Visualize a glowing ball of pure, white light and feel its positive energy harmonizing with you, bringing you into alignment with a feeling of well-being.

Now, the ball begins to spin slowly, and takes the shape of a being composed of pure white light. This shape may determine itself in your third eye, or you can assign it a shape—butterflies and birds are particularly helpful, or any animal you feel personal kinship with.

Visualize your "thought being" sitting across from you in a tranquil, sunlit space. After a moment or two, communicate with it in the following manner:

- Thank it for arising from your creative source as a defined entity.

- Give it its instructions in the form of your command sentence.

- Stipulate that it carry out the work with harm to none.

- Say *"you have the power of the Universe to draw upon and thus unlimited energy and capacity to carry out this task."*

- Instruct it to dissolve and return to formless Universal energy after the goal is accomplished, or after 7 days, whichever comes first.

Now, visualize the glowing thought form leaving your space in whatever manner is most appropriate for you. For example, if it takes the shape of a butterfly, it can flutter out the window or even out through the ceiling.

Finally, seal the work by saying *"It is done,"* or other affirming words of your choice.

CONCLUSION

Many people, when presented with the ideas surrounding the Law of Attraction for the first time, will feel excited and daunted all at once.

It's wonderful to know that we can shape our lives just by changing the way we think. Yet it's incredibly difficult, at least at first, for most of us to change how we think! So where should you even start?

The sources listed on the "Suggestions for Further Reading" page below contain further concepts, strategies and practices that can help you take what you've learned in this guide to the next level. You'll also find a few sources that can help you broaden your exploration of Witchcraft and magic, if you so desire.

But no matter what you choose as your next step, it's worth keeping in mind that you can't force a new abstract concept like the Law of Attraction to become a solid and complete framework for your life experience right away.

Integrating a new belief takes time and patience. Most importantly, it requires the practice of paying attention to the way your mind works.

As you do so, you'll identify opportunities to shift habits of thought, releasing those that no longer serve you on your path and making room for new habits that will ultimately change the way you experience the world.

This process takes different forms and occurs at a different pace for each individual, but no matter how you approach the work of changing how you think, the main thing to keep in mind is that you *can* choose where to put your mental energy.

And even when you find yourself unintentionally falling back into old habits of thought, remember that each day is a new opportunity to make a new choice that will lead you in the direction you want to go.

Keep reaching for the better choices, and you'll see new manifestations develop in your life that feel—no matter what your spiritual orientation—just like magic.

SUGGESTIONS FOR FURTHER READING

Here is a brief collection of resources you can use to expand your knowledge.

Original "New Thought" Era Sources

The original publication dates are given here for these classic books, but all of them have been reprinted in contemporary editions.

William Walker Atkinson, *Thought Vibration or the Law of Attraction in the Thought World* (1906)

Charles Haanel, *Master Key System* (1912)

Napoleon Hill, *Think and Grow Rich* (1937)

Prentice Mulford, *Thoughts are Things* (1889)

Norman Vincent Peale, *The Power of Positive Thinking* (1952)

Wallace Wattles, *The Science of Getting Rich* (1910)

Contemporary "New Age" Sources

Many of the prolific authors listed here have written a vast number of books, all of which can be useful to readers in the pursuit of mastering the Law of Attraction.

Gregg Braden, *The Divine Matrix: Bridging Time, Space, Miracles, and Belief* (2006)

Dr. Wayne W. Dyer, *Change Your Thoughts, Change Your Life* (2009)

Dr. Wayne W. Dyer, *You'll See It When You Believe It* (2001)

Dr. Wayne W. Dyer, *The Power of Intention* (2005)

Melody Fletcher, *Deliberate Receiving* (2015)

Esther and Jerry Hicks, *Ask and It Is Given: Learning to Manifest Your Desires* (2005)

Esther and Jerry Hicks, *The Amazing Power of Deliberate Intent: Living the Art of Allowing* (2005)

Esther and Jerry Hicks, *The Law of Attraction: the Basics of the Teachings of Abraham* (2006)

Joe Vitale, *The Attractor Factor: 5 Easy Steps for Creating Wealth (or Anything Else) From the Inside Out* (2005)

Witchcraft and Magic

For those who are interested in learning more about Witchcraft, including Wicca, the following books can get you on your way to a solid grounding in many basic concepts, including the Law of Attraction and much more. Some are more beginner-oriented than others, but all are worth reading no matter where you are on your own path to spiritual enlightenment.

Scott Cunningham, *Wicca: A Guide for the Solitary Practitioner* (1989)

Laurie Cabot with Tom Cowan, *Power of the Witch: The Earth, the Moon, and the Magical Path to Enlightenment* (1990)

Kala Trobe, *The Witch's Guide to Life* (2003)

Ellen Dugan, *Natural Witchery: Intuitive, Personal & Practical Magick* (2007)

Ellen Dugan, *Practical Prosperity Magick* (2014)

THREE FREE AUDIOBOOKS PROMOTION

Don't forget, you can now enjoy **three audiobooks completely free of charge** when you start a free 30-day trial with Audible.

If you're new to the Craft, *Wicca Starter Kit* contains three of Lisa's most popular books for beginning Wiccans. You can download it for free at:

www.wiccaliving.com/free-wiccan-audiobooks

Or, if you're wanting to expand your magical skills, check out *Spellbook Starter Kit,* with three collections of spellwork featuring the powerful energies of candles, colors, crystals, mineral stones, and magical herbs. Download over 150 spells for free at:

www.wiccaliving.com/free-spell-audiobooks

Members receive free audiobooks every month, as well as exclusive discounts. And, if you don't want to continue with Audible, just remember to cancel your membership. You won't be charged a cent, and you'll get to keep your books!

Happy listening!

MORE BOOKS BY
LISA CHAMBERLAIN

Wicca for Beginners: A Guide to Wiccan Beliefs, Rituals, Magic, and Witchcraft

Wicca Book of Spells: A Book of Shadows for Wiccans, Witches, and Other Practitioners of Magic

Wicca Herbal Magic: A Beginner's Guide to Practicing Wiccan Herbal Magic, with Simple Herb Spells

Wicca Book of Herbal Spells: A Book of Shadows for Wiccans, Witches, and Other Practitioners of Herbal Magic

Wicca Candle Magic: A Beginner's Guide to Practicing Wiccan Candle Magic, with Simple Candle Spells

Wicca Book of Candle Spells: A Book of Shadows for Wiccans, Witches, and Other Practitioners of Candle Magic

Wicca Crystal Magic: A Beginner's Guide to Practicing Wiccan Crystal Magic, with Simple Crystal Spells

Wicca Book of Crystal Spells: A Book of Shadows for Wiccans, Witches, and Other Practitioners of Crystal Magic

Tarot for Beginners: A Guide to Psychic Tarot Reading, Real Tarot Card Meanings, and Simple Tarot Spreads

Runes for Beginners: A Guide to Reading Runes in Divination, Rune Magic, and the Meaning of the Elder Futhark Runes

Wicca Moon Magic: A Wiccan's Guide and Grimoire for Working Magic with Lunar Energies

Wicca Wheel of the Year Magic: A Beginner's Guide to the Sabbats, with History, Symbolism, Celebration Ideas, and Dedicated Sabbat Spells

Wicca Kitchen Witchery: A Beginner's Guide to Magical Cooking, with Simple Spells and Recipes

Wicca Essential Oils Magic: A Beginner's Guide to Working with Magical Oils, with Simple Recipes and Spells

Wicca Elemental Magic: A Guide to the Elements, Witchcraft, and Magical Spells

Wicca Magical Deities: A Guide to the Wiccan God and Goddess, and Choosing a Deity to Work Magic With

Wicca Living a Magical Life: A Guide to Initiation and Navigating Your Journey in the Craft

Magic and the Law of Attraction: A Witch's Guide to the Magic of Intention, Raising Your Frequency, and Building Your Reality

Wicca Altar and Tools: A Beginner's Guide to Wiccan Altars, Tools for Spellwork, and Casting the Circle

Wicca Finding Your Path: A Beginner's Guide to Wiccan Traditions, Solitary Practitioners, Eclectic Witches, Covens, and Circles

Wicca Book of Shadows: A Beginner's Guide to Keeping Your Own Book of Shadows and the History of Grimoires

Modern Witchcraft and Magic for Beginners: A Guide to Traditional and Contemporary Paths, with Magical Techniques for the Beginner Witch

FREE GIFT REMINDER

Just a reminder that Lisa is giving away an exclusive, free spell book as a thank-you gift to new readers!

Little Book of Spells contains ten spells that are ideal for newcomers to the practice of magic, but are also suitable for any level of experience.

Read it on read on your laptop, phone, tablet, Kindle or Nook device by visiting:

www.wiccaliving.com/bonus

DID YOU ENJOY
MAGIC AND THE LAW OF ATTRACTION?

Thanks so much for reading this book! I know there are many great books out there about Wicca, so I really appreciate you choosing this one.

If you enjoyed the book, I have a small favor to ask—would you take a couple of minutes to leave a review for this book on Amazon?

Your feedback will help me to make improvements to this book, and to create even better ones in the future. It will also help me develop new ideas for books on other topics that might be of interest to you. Thanks in advance for your help!